PRESIDENT
of
POPLAR LANE

PRESIDENT
of
POPLAR
LANE

by
MARGARET MINCKS

Viking

VIKING

An imprint of Penguin Random House LLC

375 Hudson Street

New York, New York 10014

First published in the United States of America by Viking,
an imprint of Penguin Random House LLC, 2019

LIBRARY OF CONGRESS CATALOGING-IN-PUBLICATION DATA

Names: Mincks, Margaret, author. Title: President of Poplar Lane / by Margaret Mincks.
Description: New York : Viking Books, [2019] | Series: [Poplar kids ; book 2] | Summary:
Clover O'Reilly, who struggles to be heard in her large family, and comedy magician Mike
the Unusual, who only feels confident onstage, compete to become Poplar
Middle School's seventh-grade class president. Identifiers: LCCN 2018051041 |
ISBN 9780425290934 (hardback) Subjects: | CYAC: Politics, Practical—Fiction. |
Elections—Fiction. | Schools—-Fiction. | Family life—Fiction. | Magic tricks—Fiction. |
BISAC: JUVENILE FICTION / Social Issues / Friendship. Classification: LCC PZ7.1.M6315
Pre 2019 | DDC [Fic]—dc23 LC record available at https://lccn.loc.gov/2018051041

Set in Century Expanded ★ Book design by Nancy Brennan ★ Printed in U.S.A.

1   3   5   7   9   10   8   6   4   2

——○—— For Scott, Mattie, and Adam ——○——

Clover O'Reilly's
DREAM ROOM WISH LIST

PAINT (BY WALL):

* ❀ Walls one, two, and three: Eggplant Tangerine Dream
* ❀ Wall four (the Mood Wall): chalkboard paint

FURNITURE AND ACCESSORIES:

* ❀ Beaded curtains
* ❀ No bed (soooo boring)—piles of mismatched pillows
* ❀ Sewing machine for curtains and pillows (do these still exist?)
* ❀ Easel and splat mat

Dream Room Layout:

- Sketching corner
- Painting corner
- Sculpture corner
- Mixed-media corner

Miscellaneous Essential Items:

- Sewing machine (??)
- Three jars of gold glitter (at least)
- Three bottles of gold glitter glue
- Two smocks with pockets
- Palette for mixing paints
- Paintbrushes
- Molding clay
- Posters and markers for DO NOT DISTURB—ARTIST AT WORK sign (NO SISTERS ALLOWED on flip side?)

1

Clover

I took one last, deep breath. Don't worry, I wasn't about to die. It was just my last breath of roommate-oxygen. The last time I'd ever be surrounded by the smell of my older sister Violet's Vanilla Angel Rain-shower body spray.

Soon the air would be filled with another odor. (Not body odor. Ew!) The glorious odor of paint: Eggplant Tangerine Dream. It's a custom color, which means I invented it. Sometimes you can't find what you're looking for, so you have to make up something new.

If I had to wait twelve years and 150 days to get my own room, I wasn't picking some boring color off the shelf at Homer's Goods Emporium.

"Clover!" Mom yelled up the stairs.

I grabbed my Dream Room Inspiration Folder—stuffed with pictures, sketches, paint swatches, and my wish list—and raced outside.

Today would be a super great day. First, we were going to the Pancake Jamboree. If there was anything I loved as much as having my own room, it was breakfast food. Then we were going to Homer's for the paint.

Then it was only two more days till I started seventh grade. It was like a new me was blossoming from a cocoon, if cocoons had blossoms.

I love school for way too many reasons to mention, but mostly because all my friends are there. And Mike the Unusual, the cutest boy alive. Plus I'm in the Random Acts of Artness Club this year. Plus *plus*, new school supplies—crayons, sharpened pencils, notebook paper—are just so *visceral*. I learned that word from my best friend, Rachel. She reads a lot. "Visceral" means that something connects with your feelings. It's the perfect word for me because I have a *lot* of feelings.

I slid open the side door of the van and inhaled Vanilla Angel Rainshower. Violet was rubbing lotion up and down her arms. I gagged.

Sometimes having a mega-strong sense of smell can be a curse, not just a blessing. I must have a sensitive nose because I have a lot of earwax. I've read that when one sense is weak your other senses have to be extra strong to make up for it. In that way I'm kind of like Beethoven, even though I don't play the piano.

"I don't want to wear a shirt!" my little sister Daisy wailed. Baby Juniper wailed, too, because she copies everything Daisy does.

"You have to wear a shirt to the Pancake Jamboree," Dad said as he started the car.

Daisy and Juniper sat strapped into their car seats in the first row, with Juniper still facing backward. The second row was Dahlia and me.

"Pancakes are very . . . typical," Violet announced, filing her nails. To Violet, anything "very typical" is bad.

Violet got to sit by herself in the optional third row. When you're in a family with five kids, you don't get many options. But if anyone does, it's Violet. Not only does she get her own row, she's also getting her own room like me *and* she gets to wear makeup. She's not as artistic as I am, but today she had on three different colors of cat-eye eyeliner. I'm mature enough to admit it looked cool.

Honestly, I'm scared to try three eyeliner colors, because that's six chances to poke my eye out (since I have two eyes). Violet's beauty routines are dangerous. We both have curly red hair, but Violet wakes up super early to make hers straight. The last time I used her flat iron, I almost burned my hair off.

So, back to pancakes. The Pancake Jamboree is at Town Hall. We live close enough to walk, but we had to drive because we were hauling a ton of Mom's campaign signs. She was running for Poplar School Board against a man named Rocket Shipley. His real name is William, but Mom says he made up a nickname for himself so he can be "more memorable." I didn't know you could make up nicknames for yourself when you were an adult.

Clover is already a memorable name. But if I wanted to be even *more* memorable, I would be Clover "Anastasia Emerald" O'Reilly.

"Mom, are you gonna win the selection?" Dahlia asked.

"It's called a special election," I said.

"Why is it special?" she asked.

"Because a guy who was on the school board went to jail, and they have to fill his spot," I said.

Dahlia gasped. "Why did he go to jail?"

"Because he stole a bunch of money and lied," said Violet.

"If you steal and lie, then you go to jail?" Dahlia asked.

"Yup," Violet said.

Daisy burst into tears. "I don't want to go to jail," she said.

"Why would you go to jail?" Mom asked.

"I stole Violet's makeup!" she wailed. She pulled a pan of Vice City eye shadow out of her Pet-a-Pony purse.

"Oh boy," said Violet. "You'd better give it back."

"I'm not a boy!" Daisy cried even harder.

"No one's going to jail," Dad said.

"Some people go to jail," Dahlia said. "Or else jail would be empty."

"No one in *this car* is going to jail," Dad said.

"Yet," muttered Violet.

"There are different kinds of lies," Mom said. "There are little lies that don't really matter. And then there are big-deal lies."

"What's a little lie and what's a big-deal lie?" Daisy asked.

"A little lie is like when Mom told the people at Fun World you were still two so you could get in for free. Or is that a big deal?" Dahlia asked.

"It's . . . complicated," Mom said.

"I'll still vote for you, Mom," Dahlia said. "Even though you lied."

"Me too, Mommy," Daisy said.

"I'm voting for her first," Dahlia said. "In my heart."

Daisy's face turned red. She was on the verge of her second breakdown of the car ride until Mom reached back and squeezed her foot.

I rifled through my Dream Room Inspiration Folder. Dahlia snatched it right out of my hand.

"Hey!" I yelled. Magazine clippings and paint swatches scattered all over the floor, which was mostly covered in half-munched crackers and decaying French fries.

"Hay is for horses!" Dahlia said.

"Neigh!" said Daisy.

"No, *hay*!" Dahlia said.

"*No, hay neigh!*" said Juniper, clapping.

"Clover, can you take it down a notch?" Mom asked.

"Why is this my fault?" I asked. "I'm the victim!"

"Please," said Violet. I turned around to stick my tongue out at her. Like she could hear anything with her giant pink-skull headphones (which I also admit were truly awesome).

Mom rubbed her temples. Dad massaged her shoulder with his non-driving arm as he pulled into the parking lot.

Violet kicked the back of my seat. I turned around to glare at her, but the worry on her face stopped me. She nodded toward the front.

I turned back around. My parents were giggling.

Giggling is a signal. It *means something*.

"I'm starving," Mom said, rubbing her belly. Dad touched the hand on Mom's belly.

Giggles. Starvation. Belly pats.

Oh no. Not again.

Violet's eyes flashed with the same fear that bubbled in my chest.

We knew what was coming. We'd been here before. We were veterans in the Older Sister Alliance, even though Violet doesn't talk about that anymore. I guess you don't need sisters when you get to high school.

"Girls, we have wonderful news," Dad said.

I sunk down in my seat.

Violet groaned.

"We're having a baby!" Mom said.

"A *baby*?!" yelled Dahlia.

"A *what*?!" screamed Daisy. Clogged ears must be hereditary.

Juniper tried to scream "A *what*?!" like Daisy, but instead she scared herself and started crying.

"This cannot be true," I said. "You said the shop was closed for business!"

Our life was chaos already. Weren't there enough kids in this van? Did they really need more?

"It was a bit of a surprise," Mom said. "And did I really call myself a shop?"

"I need details!" I said.

"I don't," Violet muttered.

"There wasn't really a plan," Dad explained. He pulled into the Town Hall parking lot. "Aren't you guys excited?"

Wonderful. Excited. Parent code words telling me how I was supposed to feel.

"A *baby*!" Daisy screamed again.

Daisy didn't get it. She thought a baby meant good-smelling heads and goo-goo-ga-ga and (delicious) baby food for everyone. What it really meant was less of everything: time, attention, food, space . . .

"Wait," I said. "A baby needs a nursery."

"Yes," Mom said. "We'll pick out some new paint when we swing by Homer's later today."

"Nontoxic, of course," Dad said with a grin. "It'll be fun!"

Then I realized what they really meant.

"I'm not getting my own room," I said. It wasn't a question. It was a statement of absolute truth.

Mom looked at me all surprised, like it never occurred to her. "Oh! Oh, honey."

"But what about me?" Violet said.

"You can still have my office," Mom said. "As long as you don't mind my campaign stuff all over the dining room table."

Violet smiled and slipped her headphones back on.

Why did I ever think we were on the same team? Violet was on *their* team because *she* was still getting her own room. So much for the Older Sister Alliance. Second oldest meant next to nothing in this family.

"Dahlia, are you excited to move in with Clover?" Dad asked.

"You must be talking about some other Clover," I said. "Because you cannot be talking about me."

Dahlia squealed.

"Dahlia uses a heart nightlight projector," I said. "And she steals my art supplies."

"Is Dahlia going to jail?" Daisy asked.

"Maybe she should," I said.

"Find your filter, Clover," Dad warned me. He says that when I go too far or say something mean.

"Sorry," I said. Dahlia frowned, and I felt kind of bad. The new baby wasn't her fault. Sometimes when I talk without a filter, it hurts people's feelings. I'm good at a lot of things, like art. One thing I'm not good at is hiding my feelings.

But really, I don't think it's some big accomplishment if you're great at hiding your feelings. That's just more lying.

Mom turned around. I could see in her eyes that she was kind of sorry. But she also looked happy. Happy there was going to be more of us. But did anyone ask the kids who already existed what they wanted?

"Can you still run for school board when you're pregnant?" Violet asked as we piled out of the van.

"Of course," Mom said. "But there's something we need to talk about before we go inside. The baby needs to be a secret for now."

Daisy gasped. "Secrets, secrets are no fun!" she said.

"Secrets, secrets hurt . . ." Dahlia said, pausing dramatically. "My buns!"

"It's *not* 'my buns'!" Daisy screamed. "It's '*some-one*.' Secrets, secrets hurt someone."

"There's a reason I want to keep it a secret," Mom said. "A couple of reasons, actually. I'm only eleven weeks along. That's on the early side, and we want to make sure the baby is healthy." She lowered her voice. "Also, politics can be . . . difficult."

"'Difficult' means 'hard,'" said Dahlia smugly.

"Some people might think that if I'm pregnant, I won't do a good job on the school board," Mom said.

"Why not?" Daisy asked.

Mom shrugged. "It's just old-fashioned thinking. That a woman can't work if she's raising a family or taking care of a baby. That's not true, and it's not fair. But that's the way some people feel. So can we agree to keep this a family secret for now?"

She made a *shhhh* sound with her finger up to her lips.

Dahlia and Daisy did the shush-finger thing like Mom. Juniper tried, too, but she just kind of spit.

"A secret?" I said. "Don't you mean a lie? Are you going to wear tents or something to hide it?" Dad gave me the "find your filter" face without saying a word.

Maybe hiding your pregnancy is better than whatever that guy who went to jail did. But Mom was lying, too. In a way, maybe her lie was worse because I had to keep her secret, and I was her kid. How is it okay to make your own kids lie when if they lie on their own, they get in trouble? And why is it okay to lie when you're an adult? I guess it's because you're the one who gives the punishments, and it's easy not to punish yourself.

We gathered Mom's campaign stuff from the trunk and headed to the Town Hall entrance. Dad hummed as Mom's cross-body bag flopped around on his hip.

Dad always hums as a way to change the subject, to move past bad feelings like they're not even there.

"Who's ready for pancakes?" Dad asked as he pushed open the door to Town Hall.

Everyone squealed except for Violet and me. Violet didn't squeal because she probably thought squealing was typical. But I didn't squeal because my heart was breaking. I wasn't getting my own room. My dreams were as important as the litter on the floor of our minivan.

MYSTIC MAYHEM MAGIC CAMP
APPLICATION

Hear ye, hear ye!

It's time to apply. Nope, not sunscreen. Time to apply for MYSTIC MAYHEM MAGIC CAMP! The most mind-bendingly magical application will win the coveted MYSTIC MAYHEM MAGIC CAMP Scholarship. That's a free ride, my friends . . . the best kind!

This year's theme: ACHIEVING THE IMPOSSIBLE.

What You'll Need:

▶ Sunscreen (gotcha!)
▶ A pen (the kind without pigs)
▶ A video recording device
▶ Your sickest magic skillz
▶ Your most hilarious comic stylingz
▶ Anything else that ends in z

What to Do:

1. Write a 250-word essay about how you have achieved the impossible with your magic.

2. Send us a recording of YOU—yes, YOU—
performing your most impressive magic trick.

Now Let's Get Serious . . .
The Magician's Code Is No Laughing Matter!

The secrets of magic are sacred. When you share them
with a non-magician, the magic is gone. That's called "exposure." Never expose the method behind the magic, unless you're sharing your wisdom with another magician.

REPEAT AFTER ME: *"As a magician I promise never to reveal the secret of any illusion to a non-magician, unless he
or she also swears to uphold the Oath. I promise never to
perform any illusion for any non-magician without practicing the effect until I can perform it well enough to maintain
the illusion of magic."*

2

MIKE THE UNUSUAL

When you wear headphones, most people leave you alone. But not Peter Gronkowski. He keeps talking.

I sat in a white plastic chair outside the Town Hall kitchen while Peter paced back and forth in front of me. Pancakes sizzled on the griddle behind us.

Peter is my business mentor. I'm not really sure how that happened, since I didn't ask him to be my mentor. He just started giving me advice after my comedy-magic gig at his younger brother's birthday party. Now Peter's trying to help me "grow my brand."

Today's gig was part of growing my brand. According to Peter, the Pancake Jamboree was a big deal. He said I could appeal to a "new demographic." Basically, it was a chance to do magic for older kids. He got me the gig because he knows the booking agent, even though I'm pretty sure it's just the Town Hall receptionist.

The gig was a big deal for another reason. Peter was recording it for my Mystic Mayhem Magic Camp audition tape.

Last week I set out the magic camp brochure for Dad on the kitchen table, kind of like a test. I found it in the recycling bin the next day.

Dad doesn't get it. He'd rather I do basketball camp because I'm tall and skinny. He wasn't tall and skinny, so he thinks I should "take advantage."

That's why I need a scholarship, so he can't say no. But you've got to be *really* good to get a scholarship.

I think I've got a shot, because I'm not only a magician. I'm a comedy magician. Peter calls comedy my "competitive advantage," which is something that makes you stand out. Peter's the only one who knows I'm auditioning for magic camp. Not even Granberry knows.

You can do magic anywhere, but it's not the same as camp. At camp, you see people just like you. People that speak the same language.

Peter and I don't speak the same language, but we still get along. He can talk all day, and I can just nod. He doesn't care that I wear my headphones. Like always, I was listening to my favorite podcast, *Amusing Illusions*. It's the number one comedy-magic podcast in the world.

On today's podcast, Al A. Kazam was explaining the Balducci Levitation. It's a trick you do with your feet to make it look like you're floating. While I listened, I tried to read Peter's lips.

"Brad, have a lotion," he mouthed. But then he stopped talking, like he was waiting for me to say something. That's not like Peter.

I took off my headphones. "Come again?" I asked.

"Brand evolution," Peter said. "Adapt or die. As a businessman, you have to evolve to keep up with the world around you. Take me, for example." He pointed at his head. "I'm parting my hair on the other side now."

I nodded, watching the streams of pancake-hungry families pour into Town Hall.

"It's so hot!"

"So hot!"

"I'll get us a table!"

"I. Will. Not. Wear. A. Shirt!"

Clover O'Reilly's giant family walked in. They're

pretty loud, so I heard them before I saw them. They were carrying a bunch of signs with her mom's picture on them.

Some people don't have to evolve, like Clover. She fits in right where she is.

"Everyone around us is changing, even if you can't see it on the surface," Peter said. "Business tip: back-to-school is the perfect time for brand evolution." He nodded at a few kids huddled in the corner. "Did you see Jake Tripoli? Braces. That's a solid investment in his dental future. And Seema Singh got taller."

"Is that evolution or . . . puberty?" I asked.

"Both," said Peter. Just then Hannah Greer toddled through the door in very high heels.

It was weird to me that people thought they had to change just because a new school year was starting. I thought the Pancake Jamboree was about eating pancakes. But maybe Peter was right. It felt kind of like a fashion show or something, where people showed off how much they changed over the summer.

Me, I didn't change a thing. Granberry says I'm all arms and legs with a little bit of torso. I guess I grew more in all those areas. But I was still just me: Mike the Unusual, comedy-magician extraordinaire.

"I'm evolving," I said. "I'm trying out the new persona today." A persona is a character a magician plays onstage.

"Which one?" Peter asked.

"The Lovable Loser," I said. The Lovable Loser pretends to mess everything up and then wows the audience.

Peter winced. "I'm not sure 'loser' is the brand evolution we're after," he said.

Peter's phone rang. It played the sound of a cash register.

"Your stakes today just got a whole lot higher," Peter said, showing me the screen.

It was a text from Mel Chang, VIP (that's how Peter had her listed on his phone). It said, "Save me seat in ft row k thx."

"What's this?" I asked.

"Only your opportunity for fame and fortune," said Peter. "Mel's coming to review your show for her blog." I have no idea how he figured that out from her text. See? Another language. "This is it, Mike. The big time. Mel's an eighth grader now. She has pull with tweens AND teens. A five-star review from Mel is a social seal of approval."

"Oh," I said. A five-star review might also help me get the magic camp scholarship. "Well, time to suit up." That means put on my costume. Dad says it a lot. But he actually wears suits.

"I'll ping Mel back," Peter said, typing on his phone. "Terrific chat, Mike."

I walked into the far stall of the Town Hall bathroom and started my transformation.

The Lovable Loser was going to kill (that's a good thing in comedy). He's a bumbling dude who doesn't know what to say or how to act or dress. It even seems like he doesn't know how to do magic, but when you least expect it, he lands the perfect trick.

My blazer and pants were huge—on purpose— and inside out. I put my oversized shoes on the wrong feet and fastened a flower to my giant lapel. When I squeezed the flower, it would squirt me in the face. Finally, I put on upside-down glasses that I'd stomped on and taped up. I parted my curls on one side of my head and pinned a tiny hat on the other side.

Peter was right about one thing, though. The

Lovable Loser persona only works if you win in the end. What matters is whether you pull off the trick.

Before I left the bathroom, I put on my headphones. Headphones keep me in my magic mindset. Onstage, I don't need them. That's because being onstage is like being in a universe I belong to. In the real world, I need my headphones. Sometimes I feel like I'm from a different planet even though I've lived here my whole life.

On my way back to the main room, I passed two eighth graders. I pretended they couldn't see me and I couldn't see them. The magic mindset.

I can make a ball disappear in midair and vanish a coin under glass. Magic is my communication. But most people don't speak the language.

Just then I saw Granberry coming into Town Hall. She winked at me and walked over.

"Mike!" She pulled me into a warm hug, smelling like cinnamon rolls even though everything around us smelled like pancakes. "Looking sharp, kid. Just like Granbobby."

I'd seen pictures of Granbobby, so I knew I didn't look just like him. My skin is lighter, and my hair is a lot bigger. Granbobby's curls were flat against his head, and he had sideburns.

"Got your patter all worked out?" Granberry asked me.

I nodded. Patter is the stuff magicians say during their act.

Granberry was a magician, too. She was part of a traveling magic show with Granbobby: Warty Morty and his lovely assistant, Selena the Strange. Strange is our last name.

"Your dad's on his way," Granberry told me. "Coming straight from the station."

I froze even though inside my heart was jumping. I had to pull off my trick today, not just for magic camp, but to prove to Dad I was good at magic. This was the first time he'd see me perform at a real gig, in front of real people.

Maybe Granberry could tell I suddenly got nervous, because she leaned in and whispered, "Pick a card."

"Any card," I said back with a smile.

When I was little, I didn't say much. I'd only recite lines from cartoons or movies. Then one day, Granberry showed me a card trick. I started saying, "Pick a card, any card" to anyone I met. It was like how most kids might say "Hi." That's because I had words in my head that wouldn't come out of my mouth unless I was doing magic.

"Now go do your meditation," Granberry said. "And don't be *too* good! Remember Black Herman!"

I nodded. Black Herman (his real name was Benjamin Rucker) was a magician from the 1900s. He was so good at burying himself alive and pretending to come back to life that no one believed it when he dropped dead onstage during a trick.

As I walked to the stage to start my pre-show meditation, I felt a pair of small arms wrapping around my legs.

"Mike the Unusual!" Gabby Jonas yelled. "It's you!"

Peter sprinted over from across the room. "No hugging the talent," he said.

Gabby pouted.

"I'll see you after the show," I told her. She grinned. I get along great with little kids. You don't have to worry about impressing them. They don't care about brand evolution or five-star reviews. They just want to have fun.

I hung my THIS IS WHERE THE MAGIC HAPPENS sign over the stage. Then I went into a corner to meditate.

"No fans, please," Peter announced to the audience. "My client is visualizing."

I always meditate before a show. Peter calls it visualizing, but that's not the same thing. When you visualize, you imagine the future.

Meditation is about being in the present. You watch your thoughts go by, like they're floating on a stream or rolling by like cars on a train. I watched Granberry's smiling face and Mel Chang's stars travel across the hazy sky in my mind.

After a few minutes, I opened my eyes and saw Dad sitting beside Granberry.

He was wearing jeans and a T-shirt that said JUST YOUR AVERAGE STAT NERD. He didn't look like Stu the Sports Dude, sports analyst for WPOP-TV. On air, Dad always wears a suit and a tie with math symbols. But today he looked like a normal dad. Well, a normal dad obsessed with statistics.

Dad waved at me and gave me a thumbs-up. I gave him one back and smiled.

Dad's the one who looks like Granbobby in those old pictures where he's making grand gestures during a show. There's a big difference in the way Dad and I move, even the way we stand in place. I shuffle my feet and stick to the sides of a room. Dad walks straight down the middle, leaning forward like he can't wait to get where he's going.

I nodded at Peter, who was talking into a headset.

Peter took off the headset and walked to the center of the platform. When Peter walks, it's not like regular walking. He takes giant steps, like five at a time.

"Fellow citizens of Poplar, especially the honorable blogger Mel Chang," Peter said. "Fasten your seatbelts. You are in for the comedy-magic ride of a lifetime. Presenting my client . . . Mike the Unusual!"

The crowd cheered as I, the Lovable Loser, stumbled onstage (on purpose).

3

MIKE THE UNUSUAL

"Two stars," Peter said, checking his phone while wc walked back home with Dad and Granberry.

"Huh?" said Dad.

"Mel Chang's official review," Peter told him.

"What else does it say?" I asked.

"'Not very compel,'" Peter read.

"Compel?" Dad asked. "I don't know that one." He's always trying to figure out what "the kids" are saying because he wants to "connect with his audience."

"Compelling," Peter told him. "Mel always makes words shorter. It's her brand."

"What's 'compelling'?" I asked.

"It means interesting," Granberry said. She waved her hand. "But don't listen to her. Don't read your reviews, Mike, and don't believe your own press. That goes both ways, good or bad."

"You got some great You Reviews from the three-to-six-year-old bracket," Peter said encouragingly.

"You Reviews?" Dad asked.

"It's where kids leave their own reviews on Mel's blog," Peter said.

"Three-year-olds have phones?" Granberry asked.

"Koddlers are a growing market," Peter said.

"Koddlers?" Dad asked.

"Between kids and toddlers," Peter said. "A real sweet spot."

I didn't really care what Mel or the koddlers had to say. It mattered, I guess. But that wasn't the worst thing that happened today.

We stopped in front of Peter's house, which is across the street from ours.

"Peter, want to come over? Play some Battle Quest Spectacular?" Dad asked.

I tried to imagine Peter playing a video game, but I don't think he could sit still for that long.

"No thanks, Mr. Strange," Peter said. "I need to run the numbers from Mike's show to compile a detailed postmortem analysis. I'll ping you later,

Mike. Good night, all," he said, saluting us before he walked into his house.

"Ping," Dad repeated, typing on his phone.

"Did he say 'postmortem'?" Granberry asked. "Who died?"

I shrugged.

"Did you ever want to give up after a bad show?" I asked Granberry. I kept my voice down so Dad wouldn't hear.

She pulled me close as we walked up the sidewalk. "Bad shows are a magician's rite of passage. One show was so bad I threw all my props in the trash when I walked offstage. All except the livestock. But we still did the next show. And the next one. You keep going. Magic is a part of you. You don't just turn your back on magic, even when it lets you down."

"Right," Dad said, looking up from his phone. I guess he could hear us. "Everyone makes mistakes. You know the Poplar Pigeons baseball team? Once I called them the Poplar Piglets, right on the air. Mistakes like that toughen you up."

I didn't feel so tough.

———o———

The first thing you see when you walk into my house is a giant framed poster from one of Granberry and Granbobby's shows. WARTY MORTY AND HIS LOVELY ASSISTANT, SELENA THE STRANGE, TAKE OVER THE BAYOU! it says. But it's not a normal poster. My grandparents' eyes kind of follow you when you walk past it. I don't really notice it anymore, but it freaked me out when I was a kid. Beside the poster is a framed cartoon, drawn in crayon, signed ELLEN ARMSTRONG, CARTOONIST EXTRAORDINARY!

Next there's Dad's framed college degree in statistics, and a trophy case of sports memorabilia. He's got normal stuff like autographed balls and weird things like dirty socks that some pitcher wore all through the playoffs one year. And even though my parents are divorced, there's an old picture of my mom. She's grinning really big after her college soccer team won their conference championship. Now she's a trainer for a traveling women's soccer team, and she looks the same as she did back then: blonde ponytail, grass-stained jersey, and everything.

I went up to my room while Dad and Granberry started fixing dinner: pork chops, black-eyed peas, and turnip greens. I flipped on my PowerForce game system to make it sound like I was playing Battle Quest Spectacular. Really, I was shuffling cards, trying to get into my magic mindset.

Dad got me the PowerForce for my birthday last year, even though I'd asked for the Classique Comedy-Magic Gift Set. He thought it would be fun for us to play together.

My phone rang, playing the *Amusing Illusions* theme song. It was a text from Mom.

"How was the show, sweetie??" she asked. She even added little magic wand emojis.

Right now, Mom's on the road with her team. Usually I give her some details because she wants to picture it like she's there.

But today I just texted back: "Okay."

After a minute, I heard Dad through the vents. "Camille, hi," he said.

This is their pattern. Mom talks to me, and then she goes to Dad for the "play-by-play." That's what he calls it. Even though they're divorced, they get along fine.

I turned down the volume on my TV.

Dad sounded like he was reporting what happened in a game. But he was talking about me. I could only hear bits and pieces.

"It . . . all started okay," Dad said. "Scratch that. He fell down as he was going onstage . . ."

On purpose, I thought.

"And . . . audience was all little kids. Then he did that character . . . talks like he's a microphone?"

Mike the Microphone. He's been a hit since I debuted him at Clover O'Reilly's birthday party last year.

"Then the microphone said he was from a retirement home . . . I didn't get it."

The audience had laughed pretty hard at that one. I'd thought it was because I was funny.

"Then he pulled out his deck of cards."

I knew what was coming.

"Tried to do this fan trick . . . cards all over the floor. Could've heard . . . pin drop . . . his face . . . felt sorry for him. I'm worried . . . bullies."

Something strong and hot rushed through my whole body.

Dad had left something out. The reason why I failed at the Thumb Fan and dropped my cards. The reason I messed up. It wasn't bullies.

It was because I saw him checking his phone.

Maybe Mel was right. Maybe I wasn't very compel,

at least not as compel as a cell phone. I swallowed.

"Got him the PowerForce . . . like other kids . . . friends. But . . . still . . . magic . . . alone."

So that's why Dad got me the PowerForce. He wanted me to make friends.

I didn't want to be alone. That's why I wanted to go to magic camp. To find people who understood me.

But Dad wanted me to stop doing magic.

Why was sitting in your room playing video games okay but sitting in your room practicing magic was bad?

I didn't care about Mel's two-star review or You Reviews or what other kids or koddlers thought. But I didn't want my own dad thinking I was weird.

What's New with
Mel Chang

If It Trends, We're Friends.

Every year, the Random Acts of Artness Club makes a Welcome Arch to greet students on the first day of school. This year was no except.

This year's arch shimmers, prob because it's coated with glitter. I'm partic impressed by Clover O'Reilly's waving, smiling glitter cat—so chic for a seventh grader. **VERDICT:** Props to RAoA, with extra spesh props to Clover.

★ ★ ★ ★ ★

4

Clover

During the entire first week of school, everybody was talking about the awesome Welcome Arch. A five-star review from Mel Chang basically means you're a rock star. So when she mentioned my name in the review, I was pretty much set for the whole year, socially speaking. Even eighth graders said hi to me in the hallway.

It was almost enough to make me forget about losing my own room.

Almost.

School was great, but home was a disaster. Violet was moving out of our room, and Dahlia was moving in.

Now I had to deal with new roommate odors: Dahlia's strawberry lip gloss and pickles (she eats pickles with everything, so the juice gets all over her clothes). The combination was even more disgusting than Violet's Vanilla Angel Rainshower and burned hair.

Plus I was losing half my wardrobe (Violet's). Plus *plus*, Dahlia was stealing half the clothes I had left.

"Do you like my outfit?" Dahlia asked on Friday morning, spinning in front of the mirror in our room.

"Of course I like it," I said. "That's my shirt. And my belt, too. Take them off! I don't want to smell like a deli!"

"Argh," Dahlia said, throwing my shirt into a pile of dirty clothes. "Whatever. You smell like rotten syrup! And I can't go to school naked."

"Why not?" Daisy said, running topless into the room.

"Sisters are supposed to share!" Dahlia whined.

The doorbell rang.

"It's Rachel!" I yelled, racing downstairs.

I needed my best friend more than ever. If things were normal I could tell her all about Dahlia being annoying, and the unfair tragedy of losing my room, and Mom being pregnant *again*. But things weren't normal for two reasons.

One, Mom was forcing me to keep everything a secret, to protect her campaign.

The second reason was Amelia Flem.

I answered the door. Just like every other morning this week, there was Rachel (yay!) . . . and Amelia (nay).

"Hi!" said Rachel.

"Hi!" echoed Amelia.

I smiled weakly.

Rachel and I have been walking to school together since second grade. It's one of our best-friend things.

But this year, on the first day of school, Rachel brought Amelia over to walk with us. Amelia moved here over the summer. At first I thought Rachel was only being nice, that it was just some harmless first-day-of-school thing. But this was the fifth day in a row. It wasn't harmless anymore.

"*Très difficile!*" said Amelia as I lagged behind them. It's hard to fit three people in a row on the sidewalk. One person always gets pushed to the back.

It's extra hard when two of those people are speaking French.

Rachel and Amelia met over the summer. They both took a French class at the library. Their teacher, Madame Rutledge, says they're supposed to practice French "conversationally." That's super annoying because I only know, like, ten words in Spanish and zero in French except "chic," which was from Mel's review.

Today I couldn't take it anymore. "What are you guys talking about?" I asked.

"Sorry, Clover," Amelia said, turning halfway around. "We were saying how hard it is to pick an elective. There are so many good choices! What are you picking?"

"Art," I said. We had another week to pick our final elective, but I didn't give it a second thought. "What about you?"

"*Français!*" said Rachel and Amelia at the same time. Then they burst into identical giggles.

When I saw an opening, I sidled up beside Rachel.

"Here," I said, handing her a glitter-cat keychain ornament. Rachel and I exchange friendship art. It's another best-friend tradition.

"I love it!" Rachel clipped the cat to her backpack. Then she carefully pulled a piece of paper out of her front zippered pocket. She'd burned the edges to make it look old and fancy. "It's a quote."

Rachel loves reading and words, so she has a quote for almost every occasion.

I squinted at the purple ink. "*A Room of One's Own*?"

"It's by Virginia Woolf," Rachel said. "She said every great artist needs a room of her own—and money. But I don't have any money right now. Anyway, maybe you can frame it and hang it in your new room!"

"Great idea!" said Amelia.

The truth bounced on the tip of my tongue. I wanted to tell Rachel so bad. But instead I said, "Thanks."

"You should see Amelie's room," said Rachel.

"Who is Amelie?" I asked.

"Amelia," she said. "Amelie is her French name."

I wanted to ask why she picked a French name almost identical to her real name, but I didn't. I remembered my filter.

I stared at their backs while they chattered away in French. They even had matching real-bra outlines. I didn't even wear a training bra yet.

"Did you notice my pores?" I asked.

Rachel turned back. She narrowed her eyes and

peered at my cheeks. "I don't see anything," she said.

"Then it's working!" I said. "It's Violet's no-pore toner."

"Violet is Clover's older sister," Rachel explained to Amelia. "She has four sisters."

"You're so lucky!" said Amelia.

I shrugged.

"So when do you move into your new room?" Rachel asked me.

It was like she was stabbing me through the heart and twisting it clockwise and then counterclockwise.

"Um . . ." I said.

"Clover has been waiting *forever*," said Rachel. "She deserves it."

"That's awesome!" Amelia said. "I'd love to see it sometime."

I set my mouth in a straight line.

"Maybe we could have a sleepover," said Amelia. "You, me, and Rachelle."

"Rachelle?" I asked.

"Rachel," she said.

"Seriously?" But they didn't even hear me.

The trip to school took forever, like we were

walking to the real France. Finally, we turned up the corner to Poplar Middle School.

Mel Chang was standing by the Welcome Arch and waving. I turned around to see if she was waving at anyone behind me.

"Clov!" Mel called. She stomped over in her clunky black shoes. "Sick cat," she said, nodding at the keychain on Rachel's backpack.

Me. An eighth grader talked to *me*. She complimented *my* art AND gave me an awesome nickname. My skin got warm and tingly. I felt strong. Powerful.

Amelia held the front door to the school open for us.

"Thanks," I said.

"Merci," said Rachel.

They giggled.

I marched into homeroom ahead of them.

———•———

DEMOCRACY MEANS ACTION! it said on the chalkboard, in all capital letters. DO YOUR DUTY!

"Did we have homeroom homework?" I asked Rachel. "If so, I didn't do it."

"Class, take your seats!" said Ms. Adamlee, our homeroom teacher. "Now let us all rise for the pledge." She pulled out an American flag fan. "My, it's a hot one."

Ms. Adamlee has American flag accessories for every occasion. She always has something new that you never even realized came in an American flag print.

After the pledge, Ms. Adamlee carefully set her flag fan on her desk. "I have very exciting news," she said. "Today we'll choose our homeroom nominee for seventh-grade class president!"

She waited like she was expecting applause, but everyone just stared at her.

Ms. Adamlee went on. "I remember when I ran for my seventh-grade class president. Oh dear, what a lovely memory. And I would have won if it weren't for the Cobb twits—I mean twins." She shook her head. "So! Let us begin the nominations."

Scott MacGregor raised his hand.

"What does a seventh-grade class president do?" Scott asked.

Ms. Adamlee rubbed her hands. "Wonderful question, Scott! The seventh-grade class president represents the voice of the seventh grade."

"What voice?" Scott asked. "Aren't there lots of voices in the seventh grade?"

"Well, yes," Ms. Adamlee said. "That's why the seventh-grade president holds weekly after-school office hours, to hear what their classmates have to say. Then he or she passes along information to the eighth graders on the Poplar Middle School Student Council. A true representative democracy!"

"But if everyone has a different voice and different opinions," Scott said, "how can a president represent everyone? And how can you represent people if you don't agree with them?"

"Yeah, the people who win elections are just popular people and their friends," said Todd Oliver-Engels.

"That's not even a democracy," said Scott. "It's a . . . it's a . . . something else. What's that called?"

"An oligarchy," Amelia chirped. "I learned about it at my old school."

Ugh. Why did Amelia have to try so hard all the time?

"Ladies and gentlemen," Scott said, "the new girl has spoken!"

Everyone laughed. Amelia set her hands on her lap and looked down.

"It's complicated," said Ms. Adamlee. "But generally speaking, politicians are public servants. They work for you, and they should represent their voters."

"Speaking of voters, why does everyone get a vote?" Scott asked. "That's messed up. Some people shouldn't get to vote. Like Seamus."

Seamus Henry was fast asleep and drooling on his desk. Scott poked him.

Seamus bolted up in his seat. "Where am I?" Seamus asked. "Who am I?"

"Exactly," said Scott.

"What's your point, Scott?" Ms. Adamlee asked.

"In summary," Scott said, "elections are just popularity contests. It's all a joke." He folded his arms like he was a lawyer.

A popularity contest? That was a contest I could win. If I was the best artist in the school *and* president I'd for sure have *the* most power in the seventh grade. No one could replace me. Not a new baby. Not Amelia Flem. Not anyone!

"Well then," said Ms. Adamlee. "Moving on. Would

anyone like to nominate a classmate?" She stood by the blackboard, gripping a piece of American flag chalk.

Seema Singh raised her hand. "I nominate Clover O'Reilly! Clover got five stars for her Welcome Arch. That's so presidential."

Some other girls cheered. My skin tingled for the second time that morning.

"Clover?" Ms. Adamlee said. "Do you accept the nomination?"

I was so excited my shirt stuck to my chest. I sometimes have trouble figuring out gym sweat from nervous sweat from excited sweat, but I was glad I'd used Violet's deodorant today, even though she would kill me if she found out.

"So about the office hours," I said. "Do I get my own office?"

"Well, not exactly. The class president would get to use Mr. Ishizawar's classroom to listen to students' concerns."

"So if I win, can I decorate it?" Maybe my Dream Room ideas didn't have to go to waste.

"I don't know how he feels about redecorating. I . . . suppose that can be discussed," she said.

"But it's not, like, a definite no," I said.

"I suppose not? But I wouldn't pin my hopes on it. That's not why you should run for office."

It was too late. I was already redecorating Mr. Ishizawar's classroom in my head.

"Let's do this!" I said, flashing a grin at Seema.

"Scott, I assume you want to run, too," Ms. Adamlee said. "You certainly have strong opinions on the matter."

"Me? No way," Scott said. "I don't want to be anybody's public servant. I just like to argue. It's fun."

"Anyone else?" Ms. Adamlee asked.

Scott raised his hand.

"I nominate the new girl," he said. "Because she knows what 'oligarchy' means. And that seems more presidential than being good at art."

"Her name is Amelia," Rachel corrected him.

Amelia blushed. "Wow," she said. "Okay!"

"*Très bon!*" Rachel whispered. I didn't know what that meant, but it made me mad, because it sounded nice, and she should have been saying nice things to *me* because *I* was her best friend.

The class put their heads down to vote. I wanted to peek, but Rachel was behind me, and there's no way I could casually turn around to see who she voted for.

Then Ms. Adamlee spoke up.

"Clover O'Reilly is our nominee for seventh-grade class president!"

The class applauded. I smiled. I couldn't see Amelia's face because she was bent over her desk, writing in a notebook.

"And you'll get to pick a campaign manager," Ms. Adamlee said. "Just let me know by the end of today."

After the homeroom bell rang, Rachel and Amelia met me at my desk.

"Greetings, future Madame President," Rachel said. We high-fived.

"Congratulations!" Amelia said. "This is so exciting! If I can help with the campaign, let me know. I know a lot about elections."

"Thanks, Amelia," I said. "I'm pretty sure I can only have one campaign manager."

"But Amelia's really smart," Rachel said. "She's a wonk."

"A what?" I said.

"It means she knows, like, everything about politics."

I put my arm around Rachel. "But if I can pick only one person," I said, "I have to pick you. My best friend. Sorry, Amelia."

"I get it," Amelia said. "No big deal." She smiled, but her eyes looked a little darker and kind of sad.

My heart hopped around. I didn't want to hurt Amelia's feelings too bad. And maybe it would have been okay to have another person on my campaign. But the truth is, I didn't want Amelia around more than she was already. Plus she had her own gigantic perfectly decorated room.

Plus *plus*, I wanted a reason to say out loud that Rachel was my best friend. My life was changing too much already.

WARTY MORTY'S TREATISE ON MAGIC

Copyright 1973

M *Is for "Misdirection"*

If I tell you to take a left on Waverly Avenue, but a left on Waverly Avenue gets you to a dead end, what did I give you?

Misdirections.

Misdirection is the key to magic. The attention of an audience is focused on one thing in order to distract its attention from another. Managing the audience's attention is the aim of all great theater.

Sight, sound, and touch can misdirect attention. There's also my personal favorite: humor. Another time-tested misdirection method? **Patter.**

What's patter, you say? I'm not referring to the pitter-patter of little feet. No sirree, Bob! Or "I'm afraid not, Robert," if you're the more formal type. **Patter** is what you say while you perform your magic trick, like a story or a joke. Patter can enhance your performance

AND misdirect the audience. It also adds sizzle to your syntax.

Patter can be instruction: "Pick a card, any card, Andrew."

A statement: "Andrew, I just shuffled the deck" (when, alas, you didn't shuffle the deck at all! More misdirection. Sorry, Andrew).

A question: "Hey, Andrew, is your shoe untied?"

A story: "Let me tell you about the time I asked Andrew if his shoes were untied. Here's the kicker: he was wearing loafers."

What makes patter effective and engaging? Looking into your spectator's eyes. Learning your own tone of voice. And studying your own body language. What you say and do must look natural.

5

MIKE THE UNUSUAL

"Have you ever noticed," Holly Herman said, pacing in front of the classroom, "that our school mascot is the Tree Whisperer?"

"Um, yeah?" said Hannah Greer in the front row. Hannah plays the school mascot.

"If I'm elected president, I'll get to the bottom of *why* we're the Tree Whisperers," said Holly. "What does it mean? Why are the trees whispering? What are they saying?"

"Here we go," muttered Thalia Jung behind me.

When Holly went on one of her rants, it was hard to stop her. Especially when she was nominating herself for seventh-grade class president.

Holly Herman thought cafeteria workers sprinkled ground-up chewable vitamins on all the food to make the students grow extra big. One weakness of Holly's argument was that she was extremely short, and she ate more cafeteria food than anyone I knew.

But I didn't mind if Holly kept talking all day. It just meant more time for me to shuffle under my desk, out of sight of Mr. Ishizawar, my homeroom teacher. Shuffling is peaceful like meditation—that *thwap* sound when the cards hit my lap, their breeze as they settle into a perfect stack. And since Holly was talking, nobody could hear any of it. She was the perfect misdirection.

"And have you noticed the bugs in the trees?" Holly asked.

"Those nasty tree roaches?" asked Jake Tripoli. "One jumped in my backpack."

"They're not just tree roaches," Holly said. "They're spy bugs. The bugs are bugged. By Poplar Prep. They're spying on our debate team."

Mr. Ishizawar, coach of the Poplar Middle School Debate Team, looked up from his lesson plan.

"I'll also focus on environmental issues," Holly said. "Have you noticed how hot it is in here? The school's atmosphere is changing. And it's all your fault." She pointed at everyone in the classroom.

"Thank you, Holly," Mr. Ishizawar said. "Would anyone else like to throw their hat in the ring?"

Peter Gronkowski raised his hand.

"I want to issue a statement. I'm not running for office," Peter said. "I know this is disappointing. But as you all know, I'm a successful businessman. Who can forget Star Maps of Poplar Lane? Peter's Pickled Peppers? But I digress. Quite simply, a businessman should not be a politician. It's a conflict of interest. You understand."

"Thanks for that, ah, important announcement, Peter," said Mr. Ishizawar. "Anyone who *does* want to run? Or nominate themselves? Just Holly? Come on, folks. Democracy isn't a spectator sport. You've got to get in the game."

"I'll run," said Thalia. "This school is messed up."

"You want to be president?" snickered Jake. "You already got in-school suspension, and it's only the first week. Why did you bring a frog to school, anyway?"

"He was stuck in a drain, man!" Thalia said. "What was I supposed to do, leave him there?"

"You didn't have to put him on Ms. Templeton's desk," Jake pointed out.

Thalia shrugged. "I couldn't put him *in* the desk. Frogs need air."

"I'm afraid Jake has a point, Thalia," Mr. Ishizawar said. "Students who've had a recent in-school suspension are not allowed to run for office. But maybe next year."

"Whatever," Thalia mumbled, picking at her nails. "I never even wanted to be president."

"Demetrius?" Mr. Ishizawar asked.

Demetrius Doran shifted in his seat. "I don't do speeches," he said.

Demetrius is the only other black kid in homeroom. Our dads are on the same fantasy football league together. Dad really wants us to be friends, but Demetrius already has his own friends.

"Eliza?" Mr. Ishizawar asked.

Eliza Crabtree shook her head. "I can't do anything that's after school," she said. "I have to watch my little brother."

Peter raised his hand again.

"Change your mind, Peter?" Mr. Ishizawar asked.

"I'd like to nominate Michael Strange for class president."

Huh?

"Who?" said Jake Tripoli.

"Correction," Peter said. "Mike the Unusual."

Thwap. Splat.

My cards spilled to the floor. As I picked them up, I felt everyone's eyes on me.

What was Peter doing?

"Any reason why you'd like to nominate Mike, Peter?" Mr. Ishizawar asked.

Good question, I thought.

"I work with Mike closely as his mentor," Peter said. "He's loyal and fair. Even if he is uncoordinated. We're working on that. I think he'll do what's best for our school." He looked directly at me. "As your mentor, I feel politics is a natural progression for you."

It was?

"Mike, do you accept the nomination?" Mr. Ishizawar asked.

"Uh," I said.

Mr. Ishizawar said democracy wasn't a spectator sport. I wasn't so good at sports. But Dad might be happy if I did something that was kind of like a sport. And being president would look great on my magic camp scholarship application.

I nodded.

"Okay, class," said Mr. Ishizawar. "Mike or Holly. You decide."

He made everyone close their eyes for the vote. It felt weird to vote for myself since I'd never run for anything before. How could you know who would make a good president? At least Holly cared, no matter how many wacky ideas she had. Thalia might have done a good job, but she was always talking back.

I knew I'd won as soon as Holly said, "It's a conspiracy!" Then I felt a pat on my back. It was Peter.

"By one vote, Mike wins our homeroom nomination for seventh-grade class president!" Mr. Ishizawar said. "Congratulations. Who would you like to name as your campaign manager?"

Peter cleared his throat and tapped his foot behind me.

"Peter," I said. I didn't know what I was doing anyway. And it seemed like the right thing to do since he was my mentor and he nominated me.

The homeroom bell rang.

"Mike," said Peter, extending his hand. I shook it. I have a pretty firm grip because of all my card shuffling, but even my grip isn't as firm as Peter's. "I know you're a friend of the free market. Together we'll launch a complete overhaul of the Poplar Middle

School store. Take the reins on homework reform. With my fundraising know-how and your, ah, other skills, consider yourself a winner."

I nodded, though I didn't know anything about homework reform. I didn't even know we had a school store. Still, with Peter's help, maybe I could pull off my biggest magic trick yet. Mike the Unusual: Seventh-Grade Class President.

POPLAR
MIDDLE SCHOOL
Election Integrity Contract

During my campaign I agree to the following rules and guidelines:

- ★ I will use only standard-sized posters and painter's tape.

- ★ I will not attack my opponent or participate in negative campaigning against him or her.

- ★ I will not make unrealistic campaign promises.

- ★ I will not deface or remove another candidate's campaign materials.

- ★ I will behave with kindness and dignity toward my opponent.

★ I will strive to be honest at all times.

★ I will accept the results of the election
with maturity and respect.

Clover O'Reilly ❦

MIKE THE UNUSUAL
(ALSO KNOWN AS MIKE STRANGE)

WARTY MORTY'S TREATISE ON MAGIC

Copyright 1973

C *Is for "CONFIDENCE TRICK"*

Confidence is groovy, man. For magicians, it's a job requirement.

But confidence has a flip side.

The words "con" and "con artist" come from magic. Less-than-honest magicians would swindle an unsuspecting Joe or Josephine in three-card monte or a shell game. These were called "confidence games" or "confidence tricks."

A **confidence trick** manipulates the confidence, or trust, of a victim. Then the swindler swoops in for the cheat.

What's the difference between a magic trick and a confidence trick?

A magician, in many ways, uses the same technique as the con artist, just without the unhappy ending.

A magic trick is a *willing* con. Folks are in on the game. In a confidence trick, the audience has no clue they're being played for fools.

6

MIKE THE UNUSUAL

It's hard to keep a magic mindset in the Cone Zone. The bright lights, pounding music, shrieking kids, creepy animatronic ice cream cones . . . it's too much. Also, the birthday parties.

I used to have my birthday parties here. Every kid did. Except one year, only one person came. It was Peter, and he had to leave early to scout out a new location for a "business venture" (I still don't know what that means). My birthday's in February, when everybody gets sick. That's why people didn't come. At least that's what Granberry told me. It might have been true, or she might have been lying to make me feel better.

So I was dreading my Cone Zone meeting with Peter. But he was my campaign manager, and the election was in seven days. I figured I should do what he said if I was going to win.

But Peter wasn't alone. He was sitting with Scott MacGregor and a new girl I'd seen around school.

"Greetings, Mike," said Peter. He shook my hand. "Meet your dream team." He leaned in and whispered, "As your mentor, I'd advise you to remove your headphones during introductions."

I sometimes forget I'm even wearing them. I took them off. Suddenly I felt exposed. The Cone Zone lights and sounds pulsed through me.

I sat down, putting my palms flat on the table. *Focus.* "I thought *you* were my campaign manager," I said to Peter.

"The key word is 'manager,'" Peter said. His fingertips touched to make a tent. "Business tip: every great manager knows how to build a team."

The girl waved. "Hi, Mike," she said. "I'm Amelia."

"I brought Amelia on because she did a terrific job as my tutoring associate," Peter said.

"I just helped him in pre-algebra today," Amelia said. She smiled at me. "When I heard you were running, I asked Peter if I could help with your campaign," she said. "I'm kind of a wonk."

"Don't say that," said Scott. "Everyone is, um, beautiful in their own way."

"No," Amelia said. "A wonk is someone really interested in politics. It's my passion."

"What's your job?" I asked Scott. "I didn't know you cared about politics."

Scott slipped on his sunglasses. "I'm Secret Service. That's not politics. It's just cool."

"Do I need a Secret Service agent?" I asked.

"I hope not," Scott said very seriously. "But I pledge to protect you. To stand in the line of fire against milkshake or French fry attacks in the cafeteria."

"Let's get started," Peter said, opening a file folder. "I've done some research on elections. First, the person who gets the most votes wins."

"Deep political analysis, dude," said Scott.

Peter shot him a look. "Secret Service agents aren't supposed to talk," he said.

"Oh," said Scott. "Are they like those palace guards in London who can't change their expressions? I can do that, too." He went stone-faced.

"Second," Peter said, "the candidate who spends the most money almost always wins."

"What do they spend the money on?" I asked.

Peter thought. "Posters. Markers. Consultants. We need donors with deep pockets to cover all the expenses." He checked his folder. "Speaking of consultants, I have a lead on a potential consultant for the campaign." He paused. "Rafael X."

Amelia oohed. Even Scott nodded, impressed.

"Who?" I asked.

Peter sniffed. "Only the most sought-after style consultant at Poplar Middle School. He does all the big dances, Valentine's Day, back-to-school makeovers. He's even styled high schoolers."

Scott gasped.

"But he's not cheap," Peter said. "And he's so busy he's only available via SkyTime video phone chat. So we've got to raise money from donors to hire him."

Amelia cleared her throat. "I've got a few ideas, too," she said.

I nodded. She took a deep breath.

"Peter's thing is raising money. Scott's is, um, security. I'm concerned with something else."

"What?" I asked.

Amelia wiggled in her seat. "My mom's a travel nurse, so we move around a lot," she said. "I went to five different elementary schools, and this is my second middle school. Why am I telling you this?"

"I don't know," said Scott.

Peter shot him another warning look.

Amelia went on. "It's because I'm an expert in the social order."

"What's that?" asked Scott.

"The social order is how people deal with each other." She made a triangle shape with her hands. "It's a pyramid. There's the top—those are the popular people. And then there's everyone else, in different categories, below them. And when you're always the new kid like me, you get good at figuring out where everyone fits. It's basically survival."

Survival? That sounded more serious than magic camp.

"Wow," said Scott. "You really are wonky."

"What's the social order at our school?" I asked.

"Great question, Mike," Amelia said brightly. "We have some real work ahead of us. Let's start with voters. Voters come in three categories: your base, your opponent's base, and undecided voters."

"What's a base?" I asked.

"Foundation," said Peter. "It's makeup. I learned that on Rafael X's online makeup tutorial."

"The guy is a master," said Scott.

"Not that kind of base," Amelia said. "A voting base is people who are loyal to you. People who like you." She checked her notebook. "Judging by my research, Mike, you don't have a very strong base."

Ouch.

"Burn," said Scott MacGregor.

"I'm sorry," Amelia said, frowning. She really did look sorry. "We're dealing with a fundamental problem: Clover O'Reilly is popular. And you're not. I mean, you're not unpopular. You're just not as . . . electable."

Instinctively, I reached for my headphones. I felt like I was hearing Dad talk about me through the vents all over again. Maybe running for president wasn't worth hearing more bad stuff about myself.

Amelia tapped the table. "But you have a unique strength."

"He doesn't even work out," Scott said.

"What do you mean?" Peter asked Amelia.

"Think about it," Amelia said to me. "There are more of you—of us—than there are of them."

"Who is this 'us' you speak of?" Scott asked.

"Okay," Amelia said. It was like she couldn't stop wiggling. "Remember the social pyramid? It's smallest at the top. Popular people are the minority. That means the not-populars are the majority. So all we have to do is get out the vote."

"Get it out of where?" Peter asked.

Amelia sighed. "What I mean is, we have to motivate the not-popular people to vote. For Mike."

"I thought everyone had to vote anyway," I said.

"Everyone has to turn in a ballot," said Amelia. "But not everyone votes for a particular candidate, on purpose. Some people just write in a funny name."

Scott snorted. "Yeah, like Anita Tinkle."

"So electing Mike would be a disruption in the market," said Peter.

"In the social market, yeah," Amelia said.

"Terrific," Peter said.

"Why do you want Mike to win so much?" Scott asked Amelia. "Is it because Clover beat you in the homeroom election? Are you out for revenge?"

Amelia glared. "No. Not everything is about girls not liking each other. Clover picked Rachel, that's all." She looked at me. "At my old schools, I was either coming or going. I never stayed in the same place long enough to make friends or run for anything myself." She stared at her hands. "My parents say this time we're staying. So I want to be part of . . . something."

I nodded. I'd lived here my whole life, but I still didn't really feel like a part of much besides magic, and that was just Granberry and me.

"Also," Amelia said with a smile, "I want to see the underdog win."

"I thought underdogs always won," said Scott. "They do in the movies."

"This isn't the movies," Amelia said. "It's middle school. People want to be at the top of the pyramid. That's why everyone votes for popular people. They think popularity is contagious, like it's going to rub off on them."

"What do we do?" I asked.

Amelia stared at me. "We make you popular."

"Hold on," Scott said. "Then he won't be the underdog."

"It's complicated," Amelia said. "Mike starts off as the underdog. Then people relate to him, then they like him, then they vote for him."

Peter clucked his tongue. His eyes moved around like he was doing algebra in his head.

Amelia made winning the election sound like something you could control—like a science experiment. But I was the experiment. It didn't feel so good.

Still, I needed to win, to "achieve the impossible" for my magic camp essay, and to make Dad proud. And I needed my team to do it.

"A brand evolution," said Peter. "How do we do that?"

"I'm glad you asked!" Amelia said again. She unzipped her tote bag. "Rafael X is a great start, Peter. And I drew up some literature to help explain what I've seen at other schools. Best practices, cautionary tales, stuff like that." She looked at me. "Mike, the most important thing to know is that you'll be playing a character. It might feel weird. But it's only a means to an end. To victory."

"A persona," I said.

To win the election, I—Mike the Unusual, comedy magician—had to disappear.

A Brief History of Failed Middle School Elections

by Amelia Flem

SLOGANS: Bad or unfortunate slogans can sink a campaign.

- ➲ Slogans should be short, sweet, and catchy.

- ➲ Positive rhyming and alliteration are good. Penny Kent for President. Awesome Anquan = A+ Choice for President.

- ➲ But not all rhyming works. Bad rhyming: Richie Is Itchy . . . to Be Your President! (Seriously, don't rhyme just for the sake of rhyming. It doesn't end well.)

- ➲ **BEWARE THE LONG SLOGAN.** For example, Jason LeRoy: Lighting the Fires of Justice for People Who Don't Know How to Light Fires or Maybe Just Need Some Help.

- **BEWARE THE OVERLONG ACROSTIC.**
Acrostics are great for kids with short names, but for kids with long names, they're a no. Don't suffer the fate of **Michelangela Schroedersmith**, who doubled down and even insisted on doing her last name. She had to put an arrow on her poster for people to turn it over.

- **BEWARE THE EXTENDED METAPHOR.** Ryan Pump. All he had to do was leave it at Pump for President. He could have had it all with that perfect *P* alliteration. But he took it too far. He extended the metaphor. **Pump Up the Gas with Ryan** with car-shaped posters. Cute, right? Wrong. You don't put gas in a slogan. You can imagine how that went. Farting sounds followed him everywhere. (Other dangerous words: toot, flush, wipe.)

- **BEWARE THE UNFORTUNATE COINCIDENCE.** Consider the case of Gemma Killroy. Killroy for President. Classic, clean, and simple. Trouble is, she was running against a kid named Roy Ferrell. So her slogan sounded like a murder threat. The authorities got involved. Poor Gemma.

SKELETONS: Skeletons in the closet (hidden secrets)

- Minka Schwartz had a collection of overly large-eyed stuffed animals (nearly the biggest collection in the world, second runner-up). When people found out, she was toast.

- Kimball Nunes was on track to win the election. Then someone uncovered a video of him, as a kid, singing the national anthem at a swim meet. He not only cracked on the "land of the FREE" note, he strained so hard to reach it that he fell into the pool. It went viral. His campaign never recovered.

SCANDALS

- **CHEATER GATE:** Ralph Washington was living a secret double life. He asked two dates to the Winter Ball dance. After that, no one trusted him.

- **BACKPACK GATE:** Tommy Larson hired Marshall Yi to break into his competitor's backpack and steal information to win the election. At first Marshall took the fall, but a team of ragtag reporters blew Tommy's crime wide open.

- **HYPOCRITE GATE:** Sonya Grenade ran on a "Save the Earth" platform. Whenever you went to her house and drank from a soda can or plastic bottle, she'd take it from you and pat you on the back, saying, "I'll take care of it." She took care of it, all right. Her opponent busted her putting the recyclables in the regular trash.

Clover O'Reilly's

PRESIDENTIAL VICTORY PLAN

✿ Outfit: Gold glitter gown (if I ever find a sewing machine??). Violet's black shimmer platform sandals. Tantalizing Turquoise nail polish on toenails, Hippo Purple-ous on fingernails.

✿ Makeup: See Rafael X tutorial "Evening Primrose"; borrow Violet's makeup.

✿ Victory Speech: Hi! Thanks for voting for me! Um . . . ? (Rachel can write the rest.)

Miscellaneous Questions:

✿ Rainbow or gold glitter curtains for presidential office hours?

❀ Inauguration ball: yes or no?

❀ If yes, can I ask Mike to be my date, or is that awkward?

❀ If it's awkward, how awkward, from 1–10?

7

Clover

Rachel was late. Rachel was NEVER late.

I chewed the end of my glitter-paint marker and stared out my bedroom window. She was supposed to be here by now, helping with my campaign.

I pictured her walking home with Amelia Flem, taking up the whole sidewalk and giggling in French-laughter. Ugh.

To get the image out of my head, I set a sheet of white poster board on the carpet. I pressed down with my marker, and gold paint swirled out from the brush.

I breathed in the paint smell to relax.

Some artists have a muse, something or someone that gives them inspiration. I'm mostly inspired by art supplies.

I drew a large circle with cat ears and added a big smile. Right away, I knew it: the happy glitter cat would be the symbol of my campaign. My cats made people happy, and that was the goal of my art.

But I still needed a slogan for my campaign, and words are really Rachel's department.

I opened an enormous bag of sea salt caramel popcorn.

Dahlia popped up from under a pile of dirty clothes. I jumped, spilling popcorn all over my poster.

"I'm telling!" Dahlia said. "That's not one-person popcorn. It's economy size. That means it's for everyone!"

"What are you, the popcorn spy police?" I said. "Get *out!*"

"This is my room, too!" Dahlia screamed back.

I gobbled up the spilled popcorn on the poster board (the kernels without paint) and studied my glitter cat. She was Anastasia Emerald, president of the glitter cats.

"Can you believe what I deal with around here?" I asked her.

She just smiled.

"Why are you so happy?" I asked her. "You must have your own room."

"Who are you talking to?" Rachel asked. She stood in the doorway.

"My poster," I said. "Where were you?" Rachel's eyes were red. I gasped. "What happened?"

Rachel took a deep breath. "Freddy Tremble snapped my bra."

"No. Way!"

Rachel collapsed onto my giant marshmallow pillow. "It was during silent study, in English class. Out of nowhere, I'm just sitting there, and I feel this *snap*." She took a deep breath. "My bra *broke*."

I gasped again. "No," I said.

"One strap just . . . slid down to my waist. In class."

"This is terrible!" I said. "I can't handle this story! What did you do?"

"I went up to ask Mr. Carroll for a bathroom pass. And guess what happened? I'm the one who got in trouble."

"You. Cannot. Be. Serious," I said. "For what?"

"Yelping during silent study," she said. "It hurt!"

"That's disgusting!" I said. "He is *not* getting away with this."

"Amelia said it happened to her at her old school," Rachel said. "There was a bra-snapping epidemic. The girls wore backpacks all the time and walked with their backs against the walls. They even traveled in packs so they wouldn't be targets."

"Wait," I said. "You told Amelia?"

"Yeah," she said. "I saw her in the hall after class."

"Oh," I said. I wasn't glad Rachel got her bra snapped, but I was her best friend, and I should have bra-snapping story privileges.

"What happened to Freddy?" I asked Rachel.

"Nothing," she said, looking down. "Because I didn't tell on him."

"What?"

"After I got in trouble, I just . . . froze. I went back to my seat. I know it sounds weird, but I was embarrassed. Mr. Carroll's a man. I didn't want to say 'bra' in front of him."

"But why were *you* embarrassed? Freddy's the one who did something wrong!" I put my hands on my hips. "This is it, Rachel. This is my campaign."

"Bra-snapping prevention?"

"Girl power! No boy will ever get away with that stuff when I'm president!"

Rachel smiled. "I feel a little better now," she said. "And also madder at the same time! Like, so mad I know what I'm going to name the villain in my next play: Freddy!"

"Good!" I said.

"You know, it's pretty cool that you and your mom

are running for something at the same time."

"Yeah," I said, picking at popcorn kernels embedded in my carpet.

"Amelia calls your mom Wonder Woman," Rachel said.

"Why does Amelia have a nickname for my mom?" I asked.

"She volunteers for your mom's school board campaign," she said. "I thought you knew!"

I clenched a handful of kernels in my fist. "Are you for real?" I said.

"Yeah, she might be coming over here later," Rachel said.

"So Amelia wants to run for president just like me," I said. "And now she's hanging out with my mom? Why does Amelia want to steal my life?"

Rachel looked at me like I grew two heads. "I don't think it's that serious. She just wants to make friends."

"With middle-aged people?"

"She's new here," Rachel said. "And she really loves politics."

Amelia barely even knew my mom. If she did, she'd know my mom wasn't Wonder Woman, because

Wonder Woman had a lasso of truth. My mom was nowhere near that honest.

"Moving on," I said. "Let's talk about girl power. What is it exactly?"

"Other than bringing bra-snappers to justice?" Rachel asked.

"Yeah."

She chewed her lip. "Um . . . I don't really know. Just supporting girls, I guess."

"Right!" I said. We sat in silence.

"So, what do you want girls to have the power to do?" Rachel said.

"Um," I said. "Just . . . be a girl. And be powerful. "

"Yeah, but what does that mean?"

I shrugged. "Like, telling girls it's cool to be confident and go after your dreams."

"Right! And other stuff."

"Yes! Other stuff."

We sat in silence.

"Like raising your hand in class more," said Rachel. "And not being afraid to speak up for yourself."

"And not letting Scott MacGregor interrupt you when you're talking," I added.

"Oooh!" said Rachel. "You know how boys take up

the benches at lunch because they spread their legs wide open? Let's stop that."

"Awesome!" I said. I paused. "If we talk about girl power, what about the boys?"

"What about them?" Rachel asked.

"Are they just . . . left out?" I asked. "Will that, I don't know, make them mad? Or, like, offend them?"

Rachel blinked. "Equality isn't offensive!" she said. "Inequality is. If a boy is offended by that, you don't want his vote anyway."

I still kind of did, but I didn't say that. Rachel was pretty fired up.

"Can I have girl power and still like Mike?" I asked.

Rachel paused. "I think so."

"Good," I said.

"But maybe don't have a crush on him this week," Rachel said. "Because you're running against him."

"So? I can still like him. You don't have to be enemies with the person you're running against," I said. I sat up straight. "I just got the best idea ever."

"Oooh, what?" Rachel asked.

"I'm throwing a political party."

E-vite from Clover to Mike

WHO: You!

WHAT: A VERY INTIMATE "NO POLITICS, JUST PARTY" POOL PARTY! (In case you don't know, "intimate" means small and private.)

WHEN: Saturday at 11:00 a.m.!

WHERE: Clover O'Reilly's backyard!

WHY: Does politics have to be mean? We're in this together, so let's be friends! We can share supplies and make posters and stickers and stuff.

Your election buddy,

Clover

P.S. Don't forget your swimsuit!
Reply with YES, NO, or MAYBE.

Team Mike Group Text

MIKE:

[FW: Screenshot of Clover's Party
Invitation]
Uh, should I say yes, no, or maybe to
this invitation?

PETER:

Greetings,
NO. This sounds like a trap. Remember,
Rachel Chambers is Clover's campaign
manager. She likes to scheme against
me.
Best,
Peter S. Gronkowski

AMELIA:

Huh. I've never seen an invitation for a
v. intimate candidate-bonding pool party
before. 😑

AMELIA:

On the + side, we'd save $ on posters. I
think u should go, but not alone. We'll
go as a team.

AMELIA:

Who knows . . . maybe we'll catch
something exciting, like a flip-flop! 👍

SCOTT:

Will there be cupcakes? 😛

SCOTT:

Also, why are we catching a flip-flop?
Why would we catch only one? 😵

SCOTT:

What happens to the other one? 😑

SCOTT:

Unless . . . is this a shoe-throwing party?
That could be pretty sweet. 👍

AMELIA:

?

MIKE:

I only wear sneakers.

PETER:

Loafers for me. Flip-flops are unprofessional.

SCOTT:

No way. 😎

AMELIA:

Not shoes! A flip-flop is when a candidate changes their position on an issue.

PETER:

You wonks and your nonsense phrases. Anyway, we'll touch base in the a.m. and circle back tomorrow.

SCOTT:

Touch which base? First, second, third, or home? ⚾

AMELIA: 😨

How to Not Answer Questions

by Amelia Flem

Politicians have to answer a lot of questions. The most successful ones know how to do it the right way. Your goal is to not offend anyone or make anyone mad. Remember, you want votes! Here's how to get them.

➲ Answer a question with a question.

Question: Do you like pineapple on pizza?

Answer: The real question is, does pineapple like being on pizza?

➲ Ignore the question.

Question: What is your position on pineapple-topped pizza?

Answer: Have a great day!

➲ Say "I look forward to getting back to you on that."

Question: Do you plan on ordering pineapple pizza in the future?

Answer: I look forward to getting back to you on that.

● Answer another question to push your real agenda.

Question: Pineapples on pizza, yea or nay?

Answer: Thank you for your question. I believe students should have unlimited access to bathroom passes.

● Change the question.

Question: Does pineapple belong on pizza?

Answer: Does pineapple belong to the fruit family? Yes, I believe it does.

● Answer a similar question.

Question: I'm ordering a pizza. Do you want pineapple?

Answer: I enjoy pizza topped with both red and white chopped onions.

➲ Use the truth wisely (aka tell the "truth").

Question: FOR THE LOVE OF SHREDDED MOZZARELLA, DO YOU LIKE PINEAPPLE ON PIZZA?

Answer: I like pineapple. And I like pizza. Have a great day!

8

MIKE THE UNUSUAL

"I put out pizza rolls," Dad said, wiping his hands on a Poplar Pigeons dish towel. He was wearing his on-camera suit: navy, with a tie that had little numbers all over it. "Should I grab some soda from the garage?"

He folded the towel carefully on the oven handle so the logo stood out. Dad gets a lot of "swag" from working at the TV station.

When he turned his back, I shoved the towel into my pocket. Sleight of hand, just in case. I didn't really feel like explaining Dad's job to anybody.

"We're not staying here long, Dad," I said. "We're going to Clover's."

"I just want everyone to be comfortable," said Dad.

Guess who wasn't comfortable? Me.

How do you have a magic mindset at a very intimate pool party, especially without headphones? I'd also stayed up half the night trying to memorize Amelia's tips for answering questions.

When I'm onstage as Mike the Unusual, I don't have to think on my feet. I have an act, a plan. When you're talking to people one-on-one, you don't know what you're going to say or what they're going to say back. It's scary.

And questions in general are kind of a sore spot for me. They always make me feel like I'm going to answer wrong.

What made matters worse was Dad being so happy about the party. He was acting like I'd never had a friend over before. I guess I never really had, but still. He was so excited it was embarrassing.

"Is Demetrius coming?" Dad asked, arranging the pizza rolls in neat little rows.

"He's not on my campaign," I said.

"He can still come over," Dad said.

"He's not coming over."

"Well, tomorrow his dad's stopping by to watch the games," he said. "Maybe you boys can hang out with us. Or you can play something on the Power-Force."

With everything Dad said, I felt like there was something underneath: *anything but magic.*

"Aren't you going to be late for work?" I asked him.

Saturday is Dad's busy day at the station, because a lot of college sports happen on Saturdays.

Dad looked at the kitchen clock and smiled. "I can always make time to meet your friends."

"They're not really friends," I said. "Just acquaintances. Except Peter. Maybe."

We learned the difference between friends and acquaintances last year in health class. An acquaintance is when someone pretty much just knows your name. A friend is someone you can be yourself with, who knows you inside and out. Peter is probably in the middle of that. Nobody knows me inside and out except Granberry.

Just then the doorbell rang. Dad and I both went to answer it, but he got there first.

Amelia stuck out her hand toward Dad. "You must be Mr. Strange," she said. "I'm Amelia."

"So pleased to meet you," Dad said, shaking her hand. "I've heard a lot about you."

Sweat trickled down my back. I hadn't even told Dad much about Amelia, just that she was working on my campaign. But now he was making it sound like I talked about her a lot. It wasn't helping my panic levels.

"You look familiar for some reason," Amelia said to Dad. "Do you work on Mrs. O'Reilly's campaign, too?"

"You work on Mrs. O'Reilly's campaign?" I asked.

She nodded. "I told you, I love elections!"

"No, I don't," Dad said. "But . . ." He looked at me, like he was trying to figure out if it was okay to tell her. I shrugged.

"Maybe you recognize me from TV," he said. "I work on WPOP as a sports analyst."

Amelia's eyes lit up. "You're Stu the Sports Dude!"

Dad laughed. "Guilty as charged. And now I'm afraid I've got to go do my sports-dude duties. Have a compel time at the party, kids."

Amelia started squealing as soon as he left.

"This is huge! Why didn't you tell me?" she asked.

"I didn't know you liked sports," I said.

"It's not that," she said. "Your dad is Stu the Sports Dude. You have a celebrity in your family."

"So?" I asked.

"It gives people another reason to vote for you!" she said. "This totally increases your likability, Mike. Well done."

"Thanks," I said, even though I didn't do anything.

"What are you doing with your hands?" she asked me.

"Huh?" I looked down. I guess I was shuffling the air. I do that when I don't have my cards on me. Dad said I probably shouldn't bring my cards to the pool party. "Just a habit."

We moved out onto the front porch.

"Did you get a chance to look over my question-answering tips?" she asked.

I nodded. My brain still felt all twisted trying to remember everything.

"So I should try to lie . . . but not lie?" I asked.

Amelia shook her head. "'Lie' sounds really negative," she said. "I know it's confusing. I don't think a good president should lie during an election or when they're in office. But this is how we win. It's part of the game. What's the alternative? We lose and the popular people win."

"But not all popular people are bad," I said.

Clover could still be a good president even though she was popular. But I didn't say that out loud.

"Someone else deserves a chance," said Amelia. "Like you."

I wasn't sure about that. I mean, I wasn't trying

to save the world. I just wanted to go to magic camp.

"Greetings," Peter said, coming up the sidewalk. Scott was right behind him, wearing his Secret Service sunglasses.

As we walked to Clover's house, Peter slipped on a pair of rubber gloves.

"What's with the gloves?" Scott asked.

"Glitter," Peter said. "I'm allergic. And I know Clover. She puts glitter on everything."

Walking next door didn't take much time. For a minute we just stood outside Clover's house listening to the shrieks and shouts coming from her backyard.

"That doesn't sound very intimate," Amelia said nervously. "Okay. I'll handle photos and video. Hopefully we'll get some footage for our campaign-rally video. Scott's on security. Peter's on . . . glitter patrol?"

"Networking," Peter said. "And fundraising."

Amelia turned to me. "Remember, Mike . . . just say as little as possible. And try not to answer any questions."

———◦———

Amelia was right. It wasn't very intimate.

Clover's backyard was jam-packed with kids. It

looked like all of Poplar Middle School, plus Clover's siblings, their friends, and the rest of the Poplar Lane cul-de-sac.

"Plenty of networking opportunities here," Peter shouted over the crowd. He waved good-bye with rubber-gloved hands and headed into the crowd.

Clover ran over to greet us.

"I'm really sorry," she said. "I wanted this to be intimate. But somebody leaked the party to Mel Chang, and then she put it on her blog."

"Oh," I said.

"Anyway, I hope you guys brought your swimsuits," Clover said.

"Always," said Scott, pointing to his board shorts.

I was wearing mine, too, but they looked like regular shorts. Dad saw them at Garfield's department store at the mall and got one for each of us so we'd match. "They're swim trunks, but they look like real shorts!" he'd said, freaking out with joy.

Amelia and Rachel hugged and giggled something to each other in a foreign language.

Clover pulled Rachel back. "Hey, no touching the competition." Then she broke into a huge grin. "Hey, Mike, let's go check out the poster-making stuff!" She grabbed my hand.

"But you just said no touching . . ." Rachel started. "Never mind."

As Clover pulled me through the crowd, I tried to meditate in the complete chaos. I was part of it, and it was part of me. But I'd never been around this many people when I wasn't onstage before. Especially not without my headphones.

Daisy O'Reilly was yelling about wearing a bathing suit. Then Susie Lorenzo ran across the yard. *"Cannonball!"* she screamed as she jumped into the baby pool.

Glittery water splashed everywhere. Scott ducked behind a tree.

Amelia clutched her phone against her chest. "Clover," she asked, "is it okay if I take some pictures of Mike before you get started with the posters?"

Clover paused. "If it's okay with Mike," she said. Then she smiled really wide. "Wait! Take some pictures of me and Mike! Together, I mean."

"First let me check that camera for anything suspicious," said Scott, cracking his knuckles.

"It's our camera, Scott," Amelia said.

"Carry on," he said.

Clover threw one arm around me and made a peace sign with the other hand.

"This picture is going to be really special," she said. "Someday."

Someday? I coughed because I didn't know how to respond. The next thing I knew, a small, wet person smashed into my legs.

"Mike!" Gabby Jonas yelled. "Are you doing magic today?"

Gabby and a few of her friends formed a soaking wet little-kid circle around me.

"We want magic!" they chanted. "We want magic!"

"Uh," I said. My long hours of studying Amelia's question-answering tips went right out the window. I didn't see magic on Amelia's approved list of stuff to talk about.

"Mike is committed to making posters today," Amelia said.

That was a close one.

Peter was handing out business cards. He stopped when Dahlia O'Reilly walked by.

"Tell me something," Peter said to Dahlia. "Who is the *real* Clover O'Reilly?"

Dahlia pulled him under an oak tree and started whispering furiously. Peter took notes.

Clover walked us over to a picnic table covered end to end with posters, paint, and art supplies.

She'd hung a sign over it that said: HEART SUPPLIES: ELECTIONS MAKE FRIENDS!

"Heart supplies?" Amelia asked.

"Art supplies, but, like, for sharing," Clover said. "And caring." She blinked at me like there was a gnat in her eyelash.

Peter joined us at the picnic table. "I'm out of business cards already," he said. "Terrific party, Clover."

"You know this isn't a Peter Gronkowski self-promotion party, right?" said Rachel.

"Business tip: every moment is an opportunity," said Peter.

"Thanks for sharing all your stuff," I said to Clover.

"Sure," Clover said. "It's not really mine. As you know, Michael, I'm in the Random Acts of Artness Club, so I get to use the supplies. It's like a special privilege."

Peter scribbled something in his notebook. I don't think Rachel gave Clover a tip sheet on how to answer questions.

"That's a clear violation of campaign-finance rules!" Peter crowed.

"Eh, you're using them, too," Clover said. "Boys are

soooo annoying." She looked at me. "I mean, not all boys."

Peter kept scribbling.

Clover's dad came out the back screen door. "Do you guys need any lemonade?" he asked.

"No!" Peter and Rachel shouted at the same time.

"Mike?" Mr. O'Reilly asked.

He stood there, waiting for an answer. I swallowed hard and tried to remember everything on the tip sheet.

"Would *you* like any lemonade?" I asked Mr. O'Reilly.

"I'm good," he said. "How about you?"

Mr. O'Reilly was one tough cookie. He wasn't backing down.

I slightly changed the question. "Would I *like* lemonade?"

"I don't know, would you? Is this one of your routines?" he asked.

I answered a similar question. "I've had lemonade in the past and enjoyed it. I find lemonade so refreshing, don't you?"

"Yes!" Clover said. "Mike, we have so much in common!"

"I'll take that as a yes," said Mr. O'Reilly, walking back into the kitchen.

Clover cut around an outline of a giant cat head. "My slogans are 'Girl Power' and 'Clover Cares,'" she said. "What's your slogan, Mike?"

The direct questions were coming fast and furious now, like I had to duck to get out of their way.

"We have, um, many options," I said. That was a non-answer, and it wasn't even a lie. But I felt bad for not telling the whole truth to Clover since she was being so nice with sharing her stuff.

"Yeah," Clover said. "It's hard to decide. That's why I have two! Don't worry, I'll help you." Her eyes brightened. "What about 'I Like Mike!'? Because you're so likable."

"That's pretty good," said Amelia. "Thanks, Clover!"

"I changed my mind," Clover said, wrinkling her nose. "I don't like it anymore."

Susie did another cannonball, splashing me. Scott ran over holding a bandanna.

"Sorry I failed you again," he said, dabbing my cheek.

"What are you going to draw on your poster?" Clover asked, leaning so close I could smell her shampoo. It was kind of fruity but something else, too . . . pickles? Was I hallucinating odors?

I stared down at my extremely blank poster. I had to draw something, since this was a poster-making party. But I felt trapped. I couldn't even write Clover's suggestion since she didn't like it anymore.

Everyone was watching me, so I drew the first thing I could think of: an *X* with a circle around it. I think I saw it on one of my T-shirt tags. It seemed like the illustrated version of a non-answer.

"Ooooh, very abstract," Clover said. "I didn't know you were so deep!"

I shrugged.

"Now let's talk about each other's strengths and weaknesses," Clover said.

"Clover," Rachel said.

"I'll start," Clover said. "Your strengths are that you're funny. And sweet. I like your headphones."

"Really? Thanks," I said. I'd never heard anyone but Granberry say such nice things about me.

"Your weaknesses are that you can be really quiet and sometimes I don't know if you're joking," Clover said. "Your turn."

I looked at Amelia. She shook her head. I remembered a rule from the tip sheet and framed my response as a question. "Uh, you care about people?"

"I totally do! Just like my slogan!" she said, her

grin spreading across her whole face. "We are *such* a great team, Michael."

"Michael?" Rachel whispered. "And you're not on the same team."

Clover ignored her. "Michael," she said, "do you have a girlfriend?"

I almost dropped my Property of Poplar Middle School black marker. "A what?"

"A girlfriend."

The truth was I'd never had a girlfriend. I don't think I'd ever even said that word out loud before.

But before I could answer, Peter spoke up.

"He's in a relationship," he said.

I was?

Amelia glared at Peter.

"Oh," Clover said, frowning.

"Look at the time!" Amelia said. "We've got a full day of campaigning ahead of us."

"Another meeting?" Scott said. "Don't Secret Service agents get breaks?"

"We're on a schedule," Amelia said.

———⋄———

"We don't really have a meeting," Amelia said as we left Clover's house. "Mike looks a little . . . tired."

"Tired" was an understatement. I could barely see straight, walk straight, or even think straight.

"Well, my business intuition was correct," Peter said. "People hate homework. I'll play that up in my campaign-donation emails. I also spread the word about Gronkowski's Pie-Crust Cookies."

"What do your cookies have to do with our campaign?" Amelia asked.

Peter shrugged, checking his shiny green notebook. "I assembled a koddler-kid street team to get your name out there: my brother Daniel, Gabby, and Susie. They can't vote for you, but they know older people who can. And," he said, tapping the notebook's cover, "I picked up opposition research on Clover. Just in case."

"What's that?" I asked.

"A business strategy," Peter said. "They do it in politics, too. Dirt on the other side. It gives you a competitive advantage."

Amelia frowned. "Maybe," she said. "But opposition research can hurt people. You don't want to use it unless you absolutely have to."

"So . . . why did you say I had a girlfriend?" I asked Peter.

"If people know that someone likes you, they'll like you, too," Peter said. "And then they'll vote for you."

"He's right," Amelia said quietly.

"But I don't really have a girlfriend, so that's a lie," I said.

"Not a negative lie, though," Peter said.

"Yeah, maybe your fake girlfriend is the love of your life or something," said Scott. "Anyway, even if it was negative, that's what people do in campaigns, right? Like that school board ad with Rocket Shipley. He says Clover's mom has never had a real job and that's why people should vote for him." He shook his head. "Savage."

Amelia groaned. "His campaign doesn't make sense. He calls himself 'The Family Man' and then tries to make Mrs. O'Reilly look bad for raising a family. Typical politics!"

Politics was exhausting. If this was what being a politician was all about, I wasn't sure how I'd make it through a whole week of campaigning.

FROM THE DESK OF
Peter S. Gronkowski

Dear Friend,

There's a pressing issue facing everyone at Poplar Middle School. That issue is too much homework.

Imagine how your world would change if you had less homework. First, you'd have more time to start a new business in the Poplar Middle School student store. That's not allowed now, but Mike will make that happen for you. Second, you could have more time to develop the businesses you already have. Third, you could spend more time finding new customers for your businesses.

Can we count on your support? Please put money through the slits of Peter Gronkowski's locker to support Mike's campaign today.

Best,

Peter S. Gronkowski

Peter S. Gronkowski

P.S. Attached please find a coupon for 2 percent off your first purchase of Peter's Pie-Crust Cookies. Thank you for being a valued voter.

What's New with
Mel Chang

——⸙ ⸙——

If It Trends, We're Friends.

MONDAY

Today marks the offish first day of the seventh-grade class election. Obvi, today is the Meet the Candidates Luncheon.

The Meet the Candidates Luncheon is a Poplar Middle School tradish. Since 1973, seventh-grade pres candidates have broken bread with their peers to hear what's on their minds. (It doesn't have to be bread if you're gluten free.)

POPLAR POLL

If the seventh-grade election were today,
who would you vote for?

Clover: 77%

Undecided: 15%

Anita Tinkle (write-in): 5%

Mike: 3%

Seventh-grade soundbites:

🔊 "Clover for President! Her pool party had more twists and turns than a roller-coaster. It was so acrobatic it joined the circus."
—Todd Oliver-Engels (aka Big TOE), seventh grade

🔊 "I'm voting for Clover because I keep getting annoying emails from Peter Gronkowski. I'm not even sure how he got my email address."
—Mateo Medina, seventh grade

🔊 "Mike who?" —Anonymous

🔊 "Why would I vote in the seventh-grade election?" —Amber Sledge, eighth grade

9

Clover

On Monday morning, Rachel showed up on my doorstep alone.

"Amelia texted me last night," she said. "She thought it might be better not to walk to school together this week. Bad optics or something."

"Does she need glasses?"

Rachel shook her head. "No, 'bad optics' means it wouldn't look good, since she's on Mike's team."

"Oh!" I said. "She's probably right. After all, she's kind of our enemy, since she's working for Mike." I said "our" especially loud to make sure Rachel heard it.

Rachel raised an eyebrow. She'd been practicing a lot, and she'd gotten really good.

"Didn't you just throw a pool party," Rachel said, "because you said being on different teams doesn't make you enemies?"

"Yeah?"

"You're really not seeing this, are you?"

I shrugged. Rachel was kind of right, but I didn't want to say so. For some reason, even though I was running against Mike, it felt like me against Amelia. Maybe that's because I liked Mike, and I knew deep down I would probably win. In the best-friend battle for Rachel, I wasn't sure.

"Did you notice at the party that Mike didn't even mention my weaknesses?" I asked Rachel as we walked through the front doors of Poplar Middle.

"You didn't ask him," Rachel said. "You only asked for your strengths."

"Still," I said. "Pretty cool!"

"Yeah," Rachel said. "Too bad he has a girlfriend."

"Right?" I said. "I bet she goes to Poplar Prep."

I set my girl power glitter-cat posters down carefully on the hallway floor.

"Whatever," I said, unrolling my glitter tape. "It's middle school. It's not like they're getting married."

Seema Singh ran over to us, squealing. "Clover!" she said. "That glitter cat is beyond presidential. And girl power? I love it!"

She high-fived me as Mel Chang stomped by.

"G-pow!" she said, raising her fist.

"Whoa," I said. I was already making a difference, and I wasn't even president yet!

Amelia and Mike were hanging his posters in the lobby while Peter talked into a headset. Scott Mac-Gregor stood by the front doors, watching people suspiciously.

"Mike's posters aren't very . . ." Rachel looked around to make sure he couldn't hear. "Interesting."

"Yeah, I don't get them," I said. "I know he's an abstract guy. But he didn't really take advantage of the art supplies at my party."

Mike's team had taped up white posters in random places that said, WHO IS MIKE? and HAVE A ROOT BEER WITH MIKE AT THE MEET THE CANDIDATES LUNCHEON. In plain black marker. No color or glitter whatsoever. It was kind of sad, really.

"I don't even like root beer," I said. "But if it's a chance to hang out with Mike . . . hold on. Can you switch off your taste buds, kind of how you hold your nose so you don't have to smell something? That way I could drink root beer with him."

Rachel snorted. "I don't think so. And it's not a date. You're supposed to talk to voters. Plus, pretending to like root beer for a boy is, like, the opposite of girl power."

"Bummer," I said.

Later, just after fourth period, I was struggling to re-tape my glitter cat to the wall when a voice boomed over the loudspeaker.

"Clover O'Reilly, please report to the principal's office."

I heard "ooh"s and "uh-oh"s all around me. People always say that when someone gets called to the principal's office.

I snorted. There's no way I did anything wrong. The principal probably just wanted to compliment me on my campaign. Or maybe it was a secret admirer . . . OR Mike broke up with his girlfriend and sent me flowers. Or balloons! Or waffles! He knows me so well.

When I walked into the principal's office waiting area, there were no flowers or balloons. Just Poplar Middle School troublemakers.

Seamus Henry. Pepper Kowalski. Freddy Tremble. Thalia Jung. The usual suspects. They were talking but stopped as soon as I came in. I swallowed hard and sat as far away from them as possible.

A few seconds later, Pepper spoke up. "What are you in for?" she asked Seamus.

"Fell asleep again," Seamus said. "It's not my fault, man. It's so hot! You?"

"I used a remote keyboard to type on Ms. Appollonia's projected screen," Pepper said.

"Classic," said Freddy. "What did you type?"

"I am a ghost," Pepper said. They high-fived.

"What about you, Thalia?" Seamus asked, nodding at her bandaged fist.

"I got in a fight," Thalia muttered.

I cringed and tried to sink into my chair. Everyone in the hall could see me through the office's glass windows. A few people did double takes, probably wondering what I did to be in *here*.

These kids weren't like me. They cheated, lied, got suspension, and talked back in class. Nobody in here would run for class president.

The clock on the wall said it was eleven. If I had to wait much longer I'd miss the Meet the Candidates Luncheon. Not that I really needed to meet anyone. I already knew everyone. It would just be fun. And I could hold my nose and drink a root beer with Mike.

"What did you do, Freddy?" Seamus asked.

"He snapped Rachel's bra," I blurted out. The usual suspects stared at me. Oops, filter failure. But even though these kids kind of scared me, I wasn't sorry I said it. Freddy hurt my best friend.

"Nah," Freddy told Seamus. "Abusing bathroom privileges."

"Ooh," said Seamus sympathetically. "Diarrhea?"

"*No!* Hiding." Freddy looked over his shoulder. "Brayden Monk was trying to take my lunch money again."

"Wait," I said. I couldn't help myself. "*You're* in the principal's office because Brayden tried to steal your lunch money?"

"Yeah," Freddy said.

"What about Brayden?" I asked.

Freddy shrugged. "If he doesn't get me in school, he gets me on the bus."

"WHAT?" I said. "You have to tell somebody!"

Everybody laughed.

"Nobody listens to us," Freddy said. Then it hit me. Maybe these kids felt ignored . . . like me, living in a way-too-crowded house and possibly losing my best friend to a French-speaking know-it-all. They needed someone to stick up for them. If I was going to be president, I had to represent them, too.

"Freddy," Thalia said. "Did you really snap somebody's bra? That's messed up." She gave me a nod.

I half smiled, mostly because I was afraid of Thalia. She'd never really talked to me before. But I could swear we had a moment. Just then Dr. Dana stepped out to call me into her office.

"Clover," she said as I sat down in the puffy green chair across from her. "Your posters don't follow the rules of the campaign."

"What rules?" I asked.

"They're not on standard-sized poster boards. They're . . . floating cat heads. And," she said, leaning forward dramatically, "you didn't use painter's tape."

"The ugly blue tape?" I wrinkled my nose. "It doesn't mesh with my aesthetic."

"The rules for campaign materials are in the Integrity Contract," Dr. Dana said. "You signed it."

"Wait, that's why I'm here?" I asked. "For cat posters and tape? What does that have to do with integrity?"

"There's a reason for the rules, Clover," she said. "Painter's tape is important. When you peel it off, it doesn't disrupt the surface underneath."

"Cat washi tape is disruptive?" I asked.

Dr. Dana made Dad's "find-your-filter" face.

"Your *tone* is disruptive, Clover," she said. "Being president is a big responsibility. You need to be a role model for your classmates. That means not causing trouble and not breaking the rules."

My face felt all sunburned.

Dr. Dana folded her hands on her desk. "So do we have an understanding? New posters, new tape." She smiled. "Presidents shouldn't be in the principal's office."

I stood up. My blood boiled as I stormed past everyone and toward the cafeteria.

The lunch bell rang, and kids were starting to spill out into the hallway. Ugh! I'd missed the Meet the Candidates Luncheon.

I went back to the lobby, gritted my teeth, and took down my posters. The tape didn't even disrupt the wall! Dr. Dana was worried for nothing.

I didn't want to be disruptive, I just wanted to be a leader. Dr. Dana was a woman in charge. More than anyone else, she should understand.

What if the rules are silly? Shouldn't someone disrupt them?

I balled up the washi tape in my hand. Artists don't play by the rules. They break them . . . or they change them.

The Cool Candidate Checklist

by Amelia Flem

➡ Swagger/confidence. THIS IS KEY. Practice your walk.

➡ Cool clothes, especially shoes (shoes can be funky).

➡ Cool hair. Maybe a man bun? Will consult with Rafael X if we can ever afford him.

➡ Headphones are okay only if you wear them around your neck. Then you look like a DJ.

➡ Use cool slang.

➡ Be a little mysterious.

➡ Come into class after the bell rings, and don't rush to your seat. Stroll in casually and take your time.

➡ Don't wear a helmet when biking to school.

➡ Step on sidewalk cracks.

➡ Run in hallways past CAUTION: WET FLOORS signs and ignore hall monitors.

➡ Act smart but not too smart.

➡ Fail at least one quiz a week. Wave it around so that everyone knows you don't care too much about grades.

➡ Once a week tell everyone you forgot to do your homework (even if you did it).

➡ Be funny (in the right way).

➡ Do funny pranks, like turning your desk/chair backward and pretending like everything is normal.

➡ Study how to burp on command.

➡ Perfect your teacher impressions.

➡ Call a teacher by their first name.

➡ Make funny InstaVid videos in the school bathrooms (but no flush noises).

➡ Stand out but not too much.

➡ Always surround yourself with people/an entourage.

➡ Be good at sports or be friends with people who are good at sports.

➡ Be someone you'd want to have a root beer with.

10

MIKE ~~THE UNUSUAL~~

"Rafael X says the key to natural makeup is looking like you're not wearing any," said Peter. He mixed a few colors together in a pan and painted makeup on a zit near my mouth. "You're an Autumn, Mike. These colors pick up the warmth of your skin tone."

I nodded like I had a clue what he was talking about. We were in the bathroom right outside the cafeteria, in the stall closest to the window.

"How about this natural light?" Peter asked. "Rafael said it's the best in the whole school. I realize professionals don't usually put makeup on people, but it's my brand evolution. Beauty services."

We hadn't earned enough money to hire Rafael X, so Peter had been watching more of Rafael's Insta-Vid tutorials. Peter had to wear rubber gloves while he put on my makeup, so it kind of tickled. He's allergic to something called mica, and that's in a lot of makeup.

In a way, getting my makeup done was relaxing. At least it distracted me from the fact that we were getting ready for the Meet the Candidates Luncheon.

"Should we put this on InstaVid?" I asked, squinting at Amelia's Cool Candidate Checklist.

Scott shook his head. He was sitting on the sink. "No one wants to see how the sausage is made," Scott said.

I nodded, even though I didn't know if he was talking about real sausage or poop or something else.

"I brought my leather jacket for you," said Peter, nodding toward the windowsill. "Amelia said you should look cool. I wore it for my Rocks Rock! business launch last year."

Scott snatched up the jacket and looked at the label. "This is pleather," he said.

"So?" Peter said. He raised his eyebrow. "I bet you don't even have a pleather jacket."

"Bingo," Scott said. "Why would I need a pleather jacket?"

Peter glared and pressed powder on my nose. I sneezed.

"I've got something way better than pleather," Scott said, patting his overstuffed backpack. "My dad bought some Frosty Top root beer. He won't even notice it's gone till after he gets home from work. Cool, right?"

I didn't even like root beer. I remembered Amelia's Cool Candidate Checklist and tried to think of something cool to say back, but my brain froze. I looked down. Scott was wearing flip-flops, and his toenails were really long.

"So . . . so fungal, dude," I said.

"Fungal?" Scott said. "Fungal. I like it."

"Almost ready?" Amelia called from the hallway. "We don't want to be late for the luncheon."

Peter, Scott, and I packed up our bags and met Amelia. "You look awesome!" she said to me.

"I think you mean fungal," Scott said.

Amelia wrinkled her nose and shook her head. "Great job on Mike's makeup," she told Peter. "And the sandwich board is perfect! Exactly like I pictured."

My sandwich board said: I'M MIKE.

"It's a little obvious," Scott said.

"It's intentional," Amelia said. "It answers the question from the posters: Who is Mike? You're the perfect contrast to Clover. She's glitter and glitz. You're simple. No high-end art supplies. Just plain black markers."

In a 2-1 vote, my Dream Team had made an executive decision to drop "the Unusual" from my name. Amelia said she didn't want people thinking of me as too "different." I was the underdog, but I should still be familiar.

Peter was the only person who'd voted to keep it.

"I still like Mike the Unusual," said Peter, tilting his head. "It's more on-brand with his magic. Just plain Mike is boring."

"That's kind of the point," said Amelia. "That he's a regular guy. No magic." She whispered the word "magic."

I didn't feel like a regular guy, whatever that meant. What was a regular guy, anyway? Guys were pretty different. There wasn't just one kind.

"I'm not sure about the jacket," she said. "Did you bring the WPOP-TV sweatshirt?"

"On it," said Scott, pulling it out of his backpack.

I took off the sandwich board and replaced the pleather jacket with the sweatshirt. The shoulders were so big that the sleeves slumped down my arms.

"Much better!" she said, beaming. Then she

frowned. "The sandwich board covers the WPOP logo. The logo is important." She grabbed the marker and wrote ASK ME ABOUT WPOP under my name.

She clicked the cap on the marker. "Does everyone have a copy of the map?" Amelia asked. She'd drawn a map with different categories of kids and where they sat in the cafeteria. It was called "Pranksters, Traders, Outliers, and More: The Poplar Middle School Electoral Map."

Scott nodded. "I'm in the Pranksters category for sure," he said as we headed down the hall.

"You forgot to include a 'Professionals' category," Peter told her. "But I suppose I'd be the only member. I, of course, mentor many Traders."

"What category are you in, Mike?" Scott asked.

I wasn't sure. I'd never really thought of myself as part of a group before. I'm kind of off by myself. Plus, I didn't know if people really fit into categories all the time. And there's something I knew from magic: boxes. Magicians use boxes for escape. No one really wants to be in one.

Amelia answered for me. "Mike's an Outlier," she said. "They're a key electoral group. We need their support."

"What are you, Amelia?" Scott asked.

"I'm an Outlier, too," she said, looking at me. "I sit at your lunch table."

"You do?" I asked.

She nodded. "There are a lot of us. Strength in numbers."

"Why don't you sit with Rachel?" Scott MacGregor asked her. "Aren't you friends with her?"

Amelia nodded. "We're French-class friends. But not lunch friends yet."

Why couldn't people just be friends? Then again, I never even knew there were cafeteria categories.

"The cafeteria is really political," Amelia explained. "There are only a certain number of seats at a table. Once you get to seventh grade, most seats are taken. Either there's one open or there's not. And when you're new, you have to find the empty seats. Maybe someday, if you're lucky, a seat will open up where you'd like to be."

"Girl stuff is complicated," Scott said. "I know. I have two older sisters."

Amelia rolled her eyes.

I was pretty sure it was more than just girl stuff. Guys had to figure out where they fit in, too.

Scott peeked into the cafeteria. "I'll go first," he said, "to assess the situation." He whispered something into his collar and ducked inside.

"I'll set up my business cards," said Peter. "Oh, and the root beer."

"Are you ready?" Amelia asked me.

I nodded. But I wasn't. I just didn't have a choice.

"All we have to do is win over one voter today," Amelia said. "It only takes one."

I gulped.

"Where's Clover?" Scott asked, scanning the cafeteria suspiciously.

"I don't know," Amelia said. "But her not being here is great optics for us." Before we could ask, she said, "That means we look good."

Rachel was standing in a corner by the recycling bins, chewing on a pen.

It wasn't like Clover to just not show up, especially on the day of the luncheon. But I couldn't think too hard about it because Amelia was dragging me to a table in the middle of the cafeteria.

My table.

"The Outliers," Amelia said. "This table has the most unaffiliated voters."

"What does that mean?"

"People who haven't decided who to vote for yet," she said as we stopped. She cleared her throat.

Here's the thing about my lunch table. It's huge. And nobody really talks much. We don't hate each other or anything. It's just that we're united by the fact that we all do our own things. Some kids put their heads down. Other kids read comic books. Other kids doodle. Some kids actually eat lunch. I usually shuffle my cards and wear my headphones until a lunch aide tells me to take them off.

But today I felt different. I wasn't wearing head-phones. I wasn't shuffling my cards. I was just standing there, as myself. And I had to prove to Amelia, to my parents, to myself that a magician could be president. Without doing magic, I guess, since it was bad optics.

"I'm Mike," I said to the table.

"We know," said Larry Abrams. "Did you twist your ankle in gym?"

"Huh?" I asked.

"You're walking pretty funny," he said.

"Oh," I said. My ankle was fine. I'd been practic-ing my new walk on the way over. Maybe it needed some work.

"Larry Abrams has two pet chickens," Amelia whispered in my ear.

"Nice," I whispered back.

"Ask him about his chickens," she whispered. "And say their names."

"What are their names?" I whispered.

"King O'Cluck and Captain Feather Pants."

"How are your chickens?" I asked in a louder voice. "I mean, Larry Abrams, how are your chickens? King O'Cluck and Captain Feather Pants?"

"Oh," Larry said. He sighed. "They're still fighting all the time. It's hard being a chicken referee. Oh, and Captain Feather Pants ate a millipede this morning."

"That's great," I said. "I think."

Larry sipped noisily through his straw. "Hey, man," he said. "When's your next magic show?"

"My next . . . magic . . . what?" I said. I didn't know Larry knew I did magic. But I knew I wasn't supposed to talk about it. I felt like a robot starting to malfunction.

"And Hannah Greer!" Amelia announced, moving me down the line. "Hannah went to clay camp this summer."

"Clay camp?"

"It's a very specialized camp."

I nodded at Hannah. "Hannah Greer, did you enjoy clay camp?"

Hannah's face brightened. "It was awesome. Clay is, like, the most expressive of mediums." She held up a Poplar Tree Whisperer charm on her bookbag. "I made this."

"That's awesome!" I said. I meant it.

She grinned.

We stepped away so I could sip on my root beer. I closed my eyes and tried to pretend it was chamomile tea, like the kind I have with Granberry sometimes.

"I'm not sure if this is working," I said to Amelia.

"You're doing fine," she said. "Next time, do something funny."

When we got to Alan Firenza, I tried burping on command. I sounded like a dying cat, but he didn't make fun of me.

We kept going down the line. Thanks to Amelia, I learned more and more about the people I sat with every day.

After a while, it got easier. People seemed really happy when you said their names and talked about stuff that was interesting to them. Maybe all people wanted was to feel like they mattered.

"Mike!" called Peter. He walked over with Brayden

Monk. "Brayden contributed one dollar to your campaign. Isn't that terrific?"

"Sure," I said. "Thanks, dude. That's . . . terrific. Terrifically fungal."

Brayden looked confused for a second. Then he leaned down and got in my face. His breath smelled like free root beer. "Peter says you're getting rid of homework," he said.

"He'll do his best," said Peter. "Homework reform is an important part of our campaign."

"Well, you'd better," Brayden said.

Root beer came up in my mouth. Suddenly I let out a real burp.

I guess that impressed Brayden, because he snorted and shook my hand. I'm lucky he didn't break any of my bones.

"You're all right," he said. "Not like Magic Eight Ball over there."

He was talking about Alan Firenza. Alan always plays with his magic eight ball at lunch, but I barely even notice. He doesn't bother me or anyone else. I nodded, mostly so Brayden would let go of my hand.

The bell rang.

"I only got to talk to one table," I told Amelia.

"Don't worry about that," Amelia said. "You made a great impression. You're making an impact."

An impact. I'd only ever made an impact on little kids at birthday parties. But today I got to talk to kids my own age. Kids that could vote. Maybe I could be president after all.

What's New with
Mel Chang

——— ⸙ ———

If It Trends, We're Friends.

MONDAY WRAP-UP

The Meet the Candidates Luncheon was way diff than expected.

Mike's performance surprised many peeps.

"Good root beer," said Alan Firenza. "And pretty solid burp."

"That wasn't just a burp," Big TOE chimed in. "That was art *and* science. Dr. Mike earned a PhD in mouth flatulence."

Others had concerns about Mike's campaign.

"This is my public plea to Peter Gronkowski," Mateo Medina said. *"Please* stop emailing me. Or add an unsubscribe button or something. Mike's okay, but . . . Peter, man. Peter. While we're at it, why was there a creepy group of little kids waiting outside my house this morning telling me to vote for Mike?"

Rumors flew re: Clover O'Reilly's surprise absence from the luncheon.

"Why was Clover in the principal's office?" said seventh grader Holly Herman. "Her glitter-cat poster must have had a hidden camera. That's why Dr. Dana made her take it down. It just makes sense."

Other students prefer to stay out of politics.

"I think Grace Sibowitz will be an awesome president," said eighth grader Shannon Dominguez. "Wait, did you say the *seventh*-grade election? I have no clue what's going on in the seventh grade."

POPLAR POLL
Clover: 67%
Mike: 18%
Undecided: 10%
Anita Tinkle: 5%

11

Clover

When I walked into my room after school, Dahlia was drawing pickles with heart eyes all over my blank poster boards.

"Stop!" I yelled.

"We live in the same room," Dahlia said calmly. "It's community property."

"My art supplies are not community property," I said, even though I followed the community-property rule when I shared a room with Violet. "Can you please go away? I have six tons of work to do."

Dahlia put her hands on her hips. "I'm going away because *I* want to, *not* because you told me to." She ran down the hall.

I stared at the poster wreckage on the floor. I didn't have any clean posters left. How was I sup-posed to work pickles with heart eyes into my new campaign art? I pulled out my notepad to start brainstorming ideas.

Whenever I sketch, I get lost in time, so I was totally surprised when Mom called me down for dinner.

I was even more surprised when I saw Amelia Flem sitting in my seat.

"Why are you here?" I blurted out.

"Clover," Mom said, glaring at me. "Amelia was helping me work on campaign materials. She's part of my street team."

"Oh," I said. "Hi."

"You're in Clover's seat!" Daisy told Amelia.

"Sorry!" Amelia said, looking at me. "I'll move."

"Of course not," Dad said. "You're a guest. You stay where you are. Clover can pull up a chair."

Pull up a chair, in my own house? Ugh. I squeezed between Daisy and Dahlia.

Dinner smelled spectacular. We were having my favorite vegetable: green beans with bacon bits and Italian dressing.

"Please pass the green beans—*ow*!" I yelped. Daisy had just thrown an elbow in my face. Not on purpose, but it still hurt, especially for such a small arm. And no one even passed me the green beans because Juniper kept saying, "Ow!" to copy me, and everyone thought it was adorable.

"These green beans are delicious, Mrs. O'Reilly," Amelia said.

Mom smiled. "Thank you, Amelia."

Great. Amelia was sitting in my chair *and* eating my green beans.

"Amelia's been so helpful," Mom told us. "Handing out fliers, getting signatures. She's a lot like me when I was her age." She smiled at Amelia again. "Maybe someday you'll run for office!"

Hello? "I'm running for office," I said. "Right now."

Dad cleared his throat. I didn't even have to look to know he had "find your filter" written all over his face. But why didn't Mom ever talk about how *I* was like her? I'm her daughter *and* we were running for office at the exact same time!

"Clover got in trouble today," Violet announced.

"What?" I asked. "Where did you hear that?"

"Betsy's little brother saw it on Mel Chang's blog. He said you were in the principal's office with Thalia Jung."

The old Violet, the one who was in the Older Sister Alliance, would never have told on me. I fumed in my seat.

Mom raised her eyebrows. "Thalia Jung! She's trouble, right?"

I rolled my eyes. "If you must know, I broke a dumb poster rule. That's all."

"I got in trouble today, too!" Daisy crowed.

"Why?" Mom asked.

"Because I took off my shirt!"

"You have to wear a shirt, Daisy," Mom said.

"Boys can take off their shirts!" Daisy said. "It was hot on the playground. Plus Ms. Winnipeg got mad 'cause I wouldn't stand in the Ladybugs line."

"Why not?" Mom asked.

"I wanted to stand with the Beetles!"

"Isn't the Beetles line for boys?" Dahlia said.

"There are boy ladybugs!" Daisy said.

"And girl beetles," Dahlia added, chomping on a pickle. "I get it."

"Oh, and I farted during Rest and Reflection Time," Daisy said.

Dad groaned. "Daisy. Say 'toot,' please."

"Or don't say either?" Mom said hopefully.

"Why?" Daisy asked. "I like 'fart.'"

"'Toot' is cute," Dad said. "More ladylike."

"Toot is cute," echoed Juniper.

"Frankie Wilkins said 'fart,' and he didn't get in

trouble! He's not ladylike, either!" Daisy said. "*And* he takes off his shirt."

Dad groaned. "I thought girls were supposed to be easy," he said.

"Easy how?" I asked.

"Well," he said, "whenever I tell someone I have girls, they say, 'You're lucky. Girls are easy. Boys are harder.'"

"Harder how?" I asked.

Dad paused, like he was choosing his words carefully. "Girls . . . listen better. And they behave. They don't act out as much as boys. Usually."

Mom glared. Dad threw up his hands. "That's a compliment!" he said.

"But it's not," Mom said. "When you tell girls they're expected to be 'easy' or 'better,' you're making it harder for them speak up."

"I . . ." Amelia started. She wiggled in her seat. My seat. "I sometimes wonder: are girls really better behaved? Or do boys just get away with more?"

Mom nodded. "The whole 'boys will be boys' thing."

Amelia nodded, scanning the room like she was trying to see if it was okay to say more.

"Well," Amelia started. She cleared her throat. "I

mean, boys can say 'poop' and 'fart' and it's funny, but when it comes from a girl, people get . . . weird."

"There was a pooping contest in the boys' bathroom yesterday," Violet said.

"Did the boys get in trouble?" I asked.

"Yeah," Violet said. "But they also got high fives all day."

"I hope they washed their hands first," I said.

"Pooping contest," Daisy muttered, like she was setting aside a great idea for later.

"Like, can you imagine girls having a pooping contest?" Violet asked.

Violet and Amelia laughed together. I dug my fingernails into my palms.

"For girls, there are consequences," Amelia said. "When a girl gets in trouble or acts out, people talk behind her back and call her names or she gets a bad reputation. Guys get respect."

"Girls have so much drama to deal with," Violet said. "I wish I were a boy."

"I don't," I said. "Girls are awesome. Also, boys have drama, too. They have the same feelings as girls."

"That's true," Dad said. "And there are other rules for boys. Ways they're expected to act or to look cool. That's hard, too."

"They're all dumb rules," I said.

Amelia nodded. "It's pretty much impossible to follow the rules of being a girl *or* a boy," she said.

I couldn't believe I was agreeing with Amelia.

"Such a wonderful conversation, Amelia," Mom said. "I'm so lucky to have a young lady like you on my team."

That was fast. I went from semi-bonding with Amelia Flem to almost barfing in my mouth in less than a minute. If I had said "poop" and "fart" at the dinner table, Mom would not have called it a wonderful conversation. But because this was Amelia Flem, super assistant, it was totally genius?

Dad started humming.

I stood up. "Can I be excused, please?" I asked. "I'm not hungry."

———◦———

Up in my room, I looked back and forth between my glitter-cat posters, the ones I wasn't allowed to use, and the posters with the heart-eyed pickles. I thought about Daisy and how she was only in preschool but she wasn't afraid to break dumb rules.

I wanted my posters to say something meaningful, not just CLOVER CARES or GIRL POWER. I wanted them to *show* caring and girl power.

I closed my eyes to focus. The pickles with heart eyes could mean something. They could represent how girls feel like they're always being watched and judged. I decided to keep them as my background.

Then I started transforming one of my glitter-cat posters. I cut out the cat's teeth and arranged them like a crown on her head. Then I cut into her mouth. I made it wide open. Not smiling, just open, like she was talking. Loud. I pasted the cat over a pickle, with the heart eyes peeking through.

Dahlia banged on the door. "It's my room, too!" she yelled.

"Argh!" I yelled back, about to snap.

Snap.

I dropped my scissors. My posters were amazing, but I could do something else.

Snap. I pictured Freddy snapping Rachel's bra. My face felt hot from rage.

Snap. I spotted the rubber band loom Dahlia had just gotten for her birthday.

"Dahlia!" I called. "Remember what you said about community property?"

Wear Your Girl Power With Pride!

Have You Ever:

❀ Had your bra snapped?

❀ Been told to clean up art supplies after class because the boys left a mess and ran out as soon as the bell rang?

❀ Been told to eat or sit "like a lady"?

❀ Accidentally farted in class and wanted to die (but when a boy does it, it's hilarious)?

Grab a GIRLS SNAP BACK bracelet to remind yourself to snap back! I made them in every color of the rainbow, so you'll definitely find one you love.

SPECIAL MESSAGE TO BOYS:

You can support girl power, too! Did you know there are boy ladybugs? I made I'M A PROUD BOY LADYBUG bracelets just for you.

CLOVER CARES ABOUT

BOYS <u>AND</u> GIRLS!

CLOVER FOR PRESIDENT!

What's New with
Mel Chang

———— ⸲ ⸲ ————

If It Trends, We're Friends.

TUESDAY

OH SNAPPED!

Clover O'Reilly was called to Dr. Dana's office
AGAIN today. For those keeping count, and I am,
that's twice in two days.

   Pub opinion is split on her GIRL POWER bracelets.

- ◀) "Love! So presidential."—Seema Singh,
  seventh grade (sporting an enorm stack
  from the West Corridor bathroom)

- ◀) "I don't wear bracelets. It's cool there are
  guy ladybugs, though."—Seamus Henry,
  seventh grade

There were also mixed reactions to Clover's new posters:

🔊 "My cat's name is Mr. Pickles. So I really responded to the cat with the pickles. It felt like a personal message, just for me."
—Hannah Greer, seventh grade

🔊 "What do pickles have to do with cats? And boy ladybugs? It's so confusing it wrapped all the way back around to being understandable."
—Big TOE, seventh grade

🔊 "What posters?"—Frankie Hsu, eighth grade

MEANWHILE . . .

Mike cracked up his second-period history class when he burped instead of saying "present." He continues to stay busy on the campaign trail. . . .

Mike's Tuesday Agenda

by Amelia Flem

➲ Before bell: Stump speech (on top of tree stump by the flagpole)

➲ All day, between classes: Locker-to-locker canvassing of students. Hand out campaign stickers.

Lunch with special interest groups:

➲ 11:00–11:10: Meeting with the Couples/PDA Acceptance Committee

- Pro cell-phone use in school so they can send lovey-dovey texts and post couple selfies throughout the day.

➲ 11:11–11:20: Meeting with Swing Voters

- Single-issue interest group. They want to eat lunch outside by the tire swings.

➡ 11:21–11:24: Makeup touch-up in bathroom/eat energy bar/bathroom break (only if necessary!)

➡ 11:25–11:34: Meeting with Traders

- They negotiate food trades at lunch; very serious about maximum ROI (return on ingestion).

➡ 11:35: Lunch bell rings

➡ After school: Video editing for campaign-rally video in Student Media Resource Center

12

MIKE

After school, Amelia and I waited in the Student Media Resource Center for Peter and Scott. We were supposed to be picking photos for my campaign-rally video. Instead Amelia was filling me in on Clover.

"Let me give you a brief on the opposition," she said. "Clover got in trouble for her bracelets. And for sneaking into the boys' bathroom without permission."

I nodded, remembering the sound of Brayden Monk's shrieks echoing down the hallway.

"I thought the bracelets were pretty creative," Amelia said.

"Maybe I can do something creative, too." I had this idea to deliver my speech as Mike the Microphone, but I'd been scared to tell Amelia about it. Maybe she'd give me a chance.

"Too risky," she said.

I nodded.

"I wanted to talk to you about Peter," Amelia said. "His emails are . . . pushy. And his street team isn't staying on message."

"What do you mean?"

She sighed. "Daniel Gronkowski was supposed to poll voters about how much time they spent on homework each day. Instead he polled them about their favorite dog from *Canine Brigade*."

"The cartoon?"

She nodded. "Gabby threatened to judo kick anyone who votes for Clover. And Susie just asks people if they think her outfit is 'designive.'"

She shuffled through the photos I'd brought from home. They were mostly of me with my family and some of me doing magic.

"I'm worried we don't have enough raw material for the video," Amelia said. "There's not much we can use here."

"Oh," I said, looking down.

Just then Peter and Scott strolled in.

Amelia glanced at the wall clock. "The media center closes soon," she said, tapping my photos with her fingernail. "And we're missing something important for Mike's video."

"An ad for Peter's Pen Cap Replacements?" Peter asked.

Amelia shook her head. "We need a baby."

———○———

On our way to the school pickup circle, Amelia explained.

"Every political candidate kisses babies," Amelia said. "It's a thing. Ever since Andrew Jackson was president."

"Babies?" I asked. "Why?"

"Kissing babies shows you're human," Amelia said. "That you care about small, cute things. It makes people like you."

I nodded. I was so tired from campaigning that this made some weird kind of sense to me.

"Are you sure?" Peter asked, raising an eyebrow.

"Positive," Amelia said. "But we don't have much time. The media center closes in an hour."

"Isn't stealing somebody's baby . . . weird?" I asked. Maybe I was the weird one. Maybe this is what people who didn't hang out in their room practicing magic tricks did with their spare time. "What about a puppy?"

"Do you have a puppy?" Scott asked.

"No," I admitted.

"Nobody's *stealing* a baby," Amelia said, patting me on the back. "You just have to kiss one!"

I don't think I'd ever kissed a baby in my life. I'm an only child. I held my baby cousin Dylan once, but I didn't kiss him. I gave him back to his mom pretty fast, because holding an infant is stressful. They scrunch up their faces and scream a lot.

We followed Amelia around the car pickup circle. The Poplar Middle School Pops Band practice was just letting out.

"We're looking for minivans," she said. "And SUVs. Especially ones with those little sticker families on the back. Sometimes you get lucky and there's a sticker of a baby with a pacifier. Or a BABY ON BOARD decal. That's a real unicorn."

"Have you done this before?" I asked.

She didn't answer.

Tuba players, trumpeters, and drummers filed past us as we peered as best we could through tinted windows.

"We have to ask their parents, right?" I asked.

She didn't answer again.

At first I thought Amelia was just being wacky. But she looked so determined. This was getting serious.

We passed a minivan with a baby sticker.

"Aha!" said Amelia. She peered in the window and wrinkled her nose. "That's a full-grown toddler! People should update their sticker families. It's irresponsible, really."

"Isn't a toddler a baby?" I asked.

"You don't know much about politics, do you?"

None of the babies we found passed the Amelia test.

"That one has too much hair," she said. "It's practically a shrunken adult."

The next baby appeared to have a cold sore. Another one had his hands shoved down his throat.

"Teething?" Scott suggested.

"Or hand-foot-mouth disease," Amelia said seriously. "We can't take any chances this late in the game."

Finally, we reached the last large SUV in the line. This time, the window was down. In the middle row was a car seat turned backward. Amelia gasped.

"He's beautiful," she said.

The baby waved to us, practically begging for a kiss. Even I knew this was an A-plus baby. Fat cheeks, big sparkly eyes, roly-poly thighs, smiling, drooling, the whole nine yards.

We could almost reach out and touch him.

But the baby's mom was on the phone. And you can't just interrupt someone's mom when they're on the phone.

"The pants I ordered from your company have holes. *Holes*," she said. She paused. "How dare you! My home does not have a moth problem!"

"Let's try something else," I told Amelia.

"This is our last chance," Amelia said.

I wanted to tell Amelia no way. Granberry would say I'd lost my mind if she saw what I was doing. But she wasn't the one running for president. And she didn't have three new almost-friends breathing in her face, waiting for her to make a move.

"Scott, can you protect me from . . . conflict?" I asked.

Scott raised his eyebrows. "No way," he said. "I don't fight mad moms. I have my limits."

I swallowed. "I can't," I said. My words fell like a thud.

Amelia chewed her lip, looking a little panicked.

"Wait!" said Scott, running off. "I have something in my locker."

"Scott has a baby in his locker?" Peter asked.

Amelia shrugged.

We waited, watching the baby-filled minivans and SUVs pass us by.

After a few minutes, Scott came back waving a baby doll.

"Why do you have a baby doll in your locker?" Peter asked.

"For Family and Consumer Sciences class. I'm taking care of her."

"You keep her in your locker," Peter said. "Is that taking care of her?"

"I didn't say I was a great dad yet," Scott shot back. "I'm still learning."

Amelia studied the doll's face. "She looks a little pale," she said.

"Rude!" Scott said, grabbing her back.

Peter put on his rubber gloves and pulled out a container of pink powder. "Blush will help," he said. "I learned it from Rafael X's 'Healthy Glow' tutorial." He rubbed a few circles on the doll's cheeks.

Amelia looked relieved. "She's beautiful," she said.

Scott beamed like a proud father. He handed the doll to me.

"Take good care of her," he whispered.

"Let's put you guys under the American flag here," said Amelia. "Why don't you kiss her head, Mike? And, I don't know, maybe coo to her a little bit?"

For the first time in my life, I cooed. I swore I heard Scott sniffling in the background.

"You're really good at this, Mike!" Amelia said. "You're a natural!"

Natural? This was anything but natural. I was used to doing illusions in magic, but that was different. This was supposed to be real.

———•———

Later that night I ate dinner with Granberry and Dad.

"How's the campaign going?" Dad asked.

I swallowed a bite of shrimp pasta. *Great*, I wanted to say. *We almost stole a baby from a car and kissed it. But don't worry, we just put make-*

up on a doll, and I kissed that instead. Pass the pepper.

What if I did tell him? Would he still think that was better than shuffling cards in my room? I didn't want to know the answer.

"It's totally . . . fungal," I said.

Granberry started choking.

"Fungal?" Dad asked. He pulled out his phone. "I need to write that down."

Just then I got a text. I'd changed my ringtone from the *Amusing Illusions* theme to some song about being bad to the bone. I thought it sounded cool and mysterious, like Amelia said I should be.

"Pretty popular these days, huh?" Dad asked with a grin.

The text was from Amelia. "CRISIS," it said in all caps.

"I have to answer this," I said.

"Okay, Mr. Fungal," Dad said, waving me off.

"Are we talking mushroom or foot infection?" I heard Granberry ask as I headed to my room.

I called Amelia. She picked up before I even heard it ring on my end.

"We have a Peter emergency," she said. "I'm sending you a screenshot from Mel Chang's blog."

It was a picture of me, Brayden Monk, and Peter from the Meet the Candidates Luncheon. Peter was holding up the dollar bill Brayden donated to our campaign with a huge grin. Brayden had his arm draped around me like he might crush my neck.

"*Scandal,*" the caption read. "Is Mike's camp taking dirty money?"

"What does that mean?" I asked Amelia.

"Mel says the money Brayden gave Peter might have been stolen. Some other kid's lunch money. That makes it dirty." She paused. "This is terrible optics. Voters will be really upset if they know we took dirty money. It could be the death of our campaign."

Or the death of me, I thought, looking at Brayden's grip around my neck.

"So what do we do?" I asked her.

"We need to put distance between you and Peter," she said.

"What does 'distance' mean?" I said. But as soon as I said it, I already knew. I had to fire him from my campaign. The only person who believed in me when I was just a comedy magician. The only person who might actually be my friend.

"I'm sorry, Mike," she said quietly. "I'll leave it up to you."

We hung up.

Against all odds, I actually had a chance of winning. That meant going to magic camp. And Dad was proud of me. He even typed "fungal" in his phone.

I couldn't let dirty money mess that up, even though it felt worse to fire someone.

I held my breath and called Peter.

13

Clover

On Tuesday, for the second day in a row, I got called to the principal's office.

Thalia Jung was already there.

"What are you in for this time?" she asked.

"Um, I guess my rubber band bracelets," I said. "There's nothing about bracelets in the Integrity Contract. I checked! And Mike's team is giving out stickers and stuff, so it's not really fair. Also, I may have snuck into the boys' bathroom to leave the BOY LADYBUG bracelets."

"They're pretty sweet," Thalia said, holding up her wrist. She was wearing a purple-and-black one. "I've already snapped mine, like, five times today."

"Awesome!" I said. At first I was excited. I was already making a difference in someone's life! But then a group of kids passed by in the hallway. They pointed at us and started whispering and giggling.

Maybe people wouldn't vote for me if they saw Thalia wearing my bracelet. Then I thought about those girl rules Amelia mentioned. The little ones, the ones that made me worry what people thought of seeing me and Thalia together, even if we were only just talking.

We sat in silence for a second.

"What about you?" I asked. I kind of turned my head away from her, though, in case more kids walked by.

"I turned the clocks back to get out of class early," Thalia said.

"Oh." I stared at the bandage on her hand. "What happened to your hand?"

Filter failure. The question came out of my mouth before I could even think about it. Maybe Thalia and I weren't close enough for me to ask her yet. But what if we *were* that close? Was that even worse? And maybe I didn't really want to know.

"I destroyed school property," she said.

"Whoa," I said. "Did your frog, like, lay eggs in Ms. Templeton's desk?"

She laughed. I'd never heard her laugh before.

"No," she said. She leaned forward. "Here's what hap-pened."

I gulped.

"You know the machine in the bathroom that has supplies?" she asked. "For your period?"

I nodded, even though I cringed hearing the word "period." It was kind of like this forbidden thing. Most everyone knew about it, but we didn't really talk about it.

She leaned in closer. "I punched it. The machine."

"Why?"

"It wasn't working. I put in three quarters and nothing came out. So I punched it."

"Oh," I said. My face burned. I hadn't gotten my period yet.

Thalia's nostrils flared. "Yeah," she said. "I was late for class because I had to go to the nurse, and then I got in trouble again. What was I supposed to do? Tell Mr. Ishizawar, 'Sorry, the period machine was broken'? No way."

"Did the nurse help you get . . . supplies?" I asked.

She nodded. "Yeah. But why did I have to get them from the nurse? Do people have to go to her to get toilet paper? No! It's always there because people need it. So why not period stuff? And then we have to pay for it, and the machines don't even work."

The word "period" pounded in my brain. Other than a health teacher, I'd never heard anyone talk about periods so much. Part of me wished Thalia would stop saying it, because it was embarrassing to even think about. But the other part thought she was right.

———◆———

This time Dr. Dana called my parents. They weren't super happy that I'd been to the principal's office for the second day in a row, for only the second time in my life.

"This isn't like you, Clover," Dad said.

"You're running for president," Mom said. "You have to think about how it looks when your class-mates see you getting in trouble."

"Mike gives out stickers," I said. "Why can't I give out bracelets? And isn't it a good message?"

"You also went in the boys' bathroom without permission," Dad said. "And you're close to being grounded."

"Not to mention if you get in trouble one more time, Dr. Dana says you're out of the race," Mom said, crossing her arms over her gigantic cardigan sweater.

I knew she was wearing it to hide her belly, which was getting bigger every day.

I wanted to say, *I can't break dumb rules at school but you guys can lie about Mom being pregnant? Why don't adults have to sign an integrity contract?*

But I found my filter. I didn't want to be grounded. And I really, really wanted to be president, especially now that I had something to fight for.

Instead I said I'd stay out of trouble.

Then I called Rachel.

———◦———

"I'm tired of just *talking* about girl power," I told Rachel, pacing around my room. "I want to actually do something to help girls."

"Like what?" she asked.

I took a deep breath. "It's the greatest idea ever," I said. "I want to talk about periods."

Rachel's eyes grew as big as beach balls.

"Right?" I said. "I'm so impressed with myself!"

Just then Dahlia popped out of the closet.

"You said 'period'!" Dahlia said. "Ha!"

"Seriously?" I asked. "Are you ever not being a creepy spy?"

Dahlia shrugged and ran downstairs, singing, "Clover said 'period,' Clover said 'period.'"

"It's not a bad word!" I called after her.

Rachel stood up and closed the door. "I mean, what do you want to say about them? I don't get it. Also, um, you can't say the word . . ." She lowered her voice to a whisper. "Period."

"You and Dahlia are totally proving my point," I said. "Why can't you talk about periods? Boys say 'poop' and 'fart.' Those are natural bodily functions, too."

"I know, but this is middle school," Rachel said. "Do you really think boys can handle it? I'm not even sure girls can."

"I bet a lot of boys know about periods already," I said. "And if they don't, they should learn. My dad knows about them. He even got Violet flowers when she got her period."

"He sent them to school?" Rachel said, her jaw dropping.

"No, at home," I said. "Isn't that sweet?"

"It is," she said. "But not everybody wants to call attention to their period."

"Oh," I said. I'd kind of imagined a "congratulations on your period" flower delivery service at school, but I didn't tell Rachel that.

"Also, you're not a health teacher," Rachel said. "And you haven't even gotten your period yet."

"Yeah, but some girls have been getting them since elementary school!" I said. "It's like this mystery. When is it going to happen? It could be at any moment. And what if you're at school? That's scary. I don't want girls to feel scared. I want them to be prepared!"

Rachel paced back and forth in front of me. "You have to find some way to get your message across without shocking people. I think there's only one way this is going to work. And even then, it's risky."

"What?" I said.

"Janet March had something on her website once," she said. Janet March is one of Rachel's heroes. She's a famous businesswoman. "It was about how to make a message appeal to your audience."

"Like a spoonful of sugar to help the medicine go down?" I asked.

"Kind of," Rachel said, typing something into her phone. "Here it is. It's called subliminal messages."

Let's Get Subliminal!

A Janet March Guide to Subliminal Messaging

Everybody has a message, from politicians to teachers to parents. But sometimes the real message is below the surface. Massage your message with these techniques!

1. Include a brief flash of an image that will appeal to your audience.

2. Use music to set the desired mood.

3. Use repetition. When you repeat a word or a phrase, this makes the audience comfortable with what you're saying.

WARTY MORTY'S TREATISE ON MAGIC

Copyright 1973

V *Is for "Ventriloquism"*

A ventriloquist speaks without moving his lips, so his voice seems like it's coming from somewhere else. A lot of folks use puppets or wooden dummies to practice ventriloquism, which is also called "throwing your voice."

To throw your voice, you need to do two things:

1. Speak without moving your lips.

2. Make your voice seem distant, like it's coming from somewhere else.

FUN FACT-O-RAMA

The first successful American-born ventriloquist was Richard Potter, a black man born in 1783. (Many magicians say that he's the first professional American-born magician, period!)

What's New with
Mel Chang

—— 3 ε ——

If It Trends, We're Friends.

WEDNESDAY

PETER GRONKOWSKI OUT

Mike's campaign has offish dumped seventh-grade businessman Peter Gronkowski after the dirty money scandal.

In a statement, PG said, "I resigned from Mike's campaign to spend more time with my businesses. Look out for Peter's Pocket Warmers later this month."

Peter's exit pleased one voter. "Does that mean . . . no more emails?" asked Mateo Medina, his eyes filling with happy tears. "No more kids outside my house threatening to judo kick me? YES! MIKE FOR PRESIDENT!"

MEANWHILE . . .

Despite Mike's crisis, Clover O'Reilly's poss connections to known prankster Thalia Jung leave her on shaky ground. Watch for fireworks at the campaign rally this aft, in the gym.

POPLAR POLL
Clover: 50%
Mike: 42%
Anita Tinkle 5%
Undecided: 3%

14

Clover

The gym was packed for the rally. The Poplar Middle School Pops Band played the school song:

Over the treetops and 'round the bend,
Poplar Middle School is a friend till the end.
It's our school spirit that sets us apart,
A whole lot of joy and a whole lot of . . . *heart*!

Hardly anyone was singing. Most kids were laughing or shouting "*fart*" at the "*heart*" part of the song.

Dr. Dana tapped the microphone and cleared her throat.

"Today's video rally is for the candidates to show you, in their own words, what they stand for," she said. "We'll go in alphabetical order. First we have . . . Clover O'Reilly."

I jumped up. "Here I go!" I squealed to Rachel. "I can't wait for you to see it. Don't worry, I super-massaged the message."

Rachel had had to leave early last night to study for a French quiz with Amelia. But I knew she'd love the video, because I'd followed Janet March's directions to a tee.

The video started with a cool song I made up myself on the computer. The word "Clover" exploded on the screen in a cloud of gold glitter.

The audience oohed and aahed.

When the glitter faded, there was a stop-motion animated glitter cat behind it. The frame pulled out to reveal a whole line of glitter cats. They were doing a kick line like the Rockettes, saying, "Clover for President!"

I heard some applause. Even Rachel was smiling.

One of the backup-dancer glitter cats tilted her head.

"Who are you voting for?" she asked the head glitter cat.

The head glitter cat looked at the camera. "Clover. Period," she said.

Underneath the voiceover I'd put in a subliminal audio message: "Bathrooms. Bathrooms. Bathrooms."

"Is something wrong with the sound?" Rachel asked. "Weird. Suddenly I have to pee."

"Everything sounds great to me!" I said. Even my subliminal messages were working!

I'd put in a super-fast image of a monster truck, to show something that appealed to boys. I even added a subliminal fart sound to make the message extra boy-friendly. But I guess it wasn't very subliminal, because Rachel poked me and said, "Was that a farting truck?"

I shrugged.

The animated glitter cats came back.

"Clover is cool. Period," said the head glitter cat. Every cat down the line repeated, "Period!"

"Does that count as subliminal?" Rachel asked.

"It's a double meaning," I said. "AND it's using repetition. Very effective." I'd even given the cats both boy and girl voices to massage the message even more.

But suddenly the main music cut off. All you could hear was the message underneath, which was definitely not subliminal. "Natural. Beautiful. Natural. Beautiful."

"Huh?" Rachel said.

It got worse. I'd tried to squeeze in an image of

a cool-looking guy kicking a soccer ball, but the dancing-cat layer of the video didn't go away, so it just looked like the guy was kicking the cats.

"This is just disturbing," said Rachel. "Not natural OR beautiful."

"I've never done subliminal messages, okay?" I hissed. "Everyone makes mistakes!"

Then my face popped onto the screen. What I'd really said was, "Hi, I'm Clover. As president, I want you to say the word 'period.' Period!"

But with the audio all messed up, you couldn't hear any of my real message, just a repeating loop of fart sounds.

Oh. No.

My video was a disaster.

15

MIKE

The auditorium went dead quiet after Clover's video. Then a lot of kids started cracking up. A few people applauded, but not at the same time.

"What just happened?" I whispered to Amelia.

She shook her head. "I've seen a lot of weird campaign stuff. But that might be the weirdest. Even weirder than Tatum Tolliver doing a blindfolded interpretive dance instead of a speech."

I scanned the crowd and saw Peter. He was sitting by himself, wearing his phone headset but not talking. Maybe they were like headphones to him. A way to get through a hard time. And I was the one who'd made things hard.

My shoulders tensed up. I wanted to use the Balducci Levitation and float right out of the auditorium.

But Dr. Dana walked up to the microphone to introduce me.

"FYI, I cut out the part with the fake baby," Amelia whispered.

"Good," I said, relaxing a little. The doll thing was pretty fake and cheesy. Also, last night I'd had a nightmare about being chased by an army of screaming, makeup-faced koddlers.

"Don't worry," she said. "I have something *way* better!"

Dr. Dana tapped the microphone. "Well, Clover, that was . . . interesting," she said. "Now let's hear from Mike."

I sat up straight. I hadn't seen one frame of a video that was supposed to be all about me, but I had to trust my team.

The video started with a picture of Dad.

Huh?

"Meet Mike's dad," said the voiceover.

"That dude looks familiar," someone in the audience said.

"Dude!" said someone else. "It's Stu the Sports Dude!"

The crowd gasped.

"No way!"

"That's Mike's dad?"

"Awesome!"

There was a series of shots of Dad at the news station, shaking hands with baseball players and basketball players.

"I've known Mike since . . . well, since the day he was born," Dad said in a voiceover.

There was a picture of Dad in a doctor's mask, holding me as a newborn.

"Awwwww," Scott whispered behind me.

"Mike's always been cool," Dad said in the video. "A really fungal dude. He likes to hang out."

There were more pictures of Dad on set at WPOP, talking to famous athletes.

There was Dad telling a joke on the air. "Why do teenagers travel in packs of three?" he asked. "Because they can't even."

There was Dad kicking a soccer ball with Ethan Jackson, the kid from Poplar High who went pro.

There was even Dad eating ice cream at the Cone Zone with Peter's street team kids. Peter had tried to make them look like cool, older athletes by putting them in makeup and tracksuits, but Daniel was still wearing his leprechaun hat. I could tell they were sitting on stacks of books to look taller.

"Is this just . . . pictures of my dad?" I asked.

Amelia nodded as another picture flashed of Dad with his barber. "Isn't it great? He was so excited to help!"

Amelia hadn't used any of the pictures I'd given her. Like the ones with me and Granberry working on puzzles together. I guess they weren't exciting enough for the video.

Suddenly the music stopped. The screen went black, and some words came up, right beside the WPOP logo:

"Mike for President. Endorsed by STU the SPORTS DUDE."

The crowd went wild.

————•————

Amelia's eyes were shining as we left the gym. "Did you love it?" she asked me. "It was magical. Your dad did such a great job!"

I pretended to look at something behind me so she wouldn't see my face. This version of me—the kid Dad talked about, the fungal kid who hung out and didn't do magic—that's who he really wanted. Not the kid he actually got. That's who my team wanted, too. And it made me dizzy if I thought too hard about it. That I wasn't good enough the way I was.

My stomach turned. The video was supposed to be about me, and I wasn't even in it, other than some picture of me as a newborn. It felt like a trick, and not the good kind. Like one of those con games I read about in *Warty Morty's Treatise on Magic*. The audience became victims, and we were the con artists.

Amelia handed me an envelope.

"This is from Peter," she said.

"What is it?"

"Money he raised for the campaign," she said. "And he gave Brayden the dollar back. Brayden was pretty mad, but Peter said he'd handle it."

I looked for Peter in the stands again, but he'd already left.

"What do we do with the money?" I asked.

"We can donate it to the school or give it back to the kids who donated," she said. "It's not that much. Peter gave it to me so no one would see you talking to him. He didn't want any bad optics." She paused. "He's a pretty good guy."

"Yeah," I said. "He is."

I opened the envelope. Inside was just three dollars and a list of people they came from. "Good luck, Mike," said the note. "Best, Peter."

I know Peter signed everything with "Best," but I think he really did want the best for me. Okay, he also wanted to sell his stuff in the school store and get rid of homework so he could spend more time on his businesses. But in his heart, I knew Peter just wanted me to get something I'd never had from kids our age: respect. He was trying to help because he was my friend.

Was.

I closed my eyes, trying hard to disappear into my magic mindset. I didn't want to be president anymore, but I couldn't drop out. Not with a whole auditorium and my team and Dad counting on me. And what about magic camp?

I couldn't drop out, but I couldn't win, either. So I had to figure out how to lose.

What's New with
Mel Chang

———— 3 ? ————

If It Trends, We're Friends.

FILE UNDER: WHOA

For the first time ever, Mike is LEADING in the polls! IKR?

- 🔊 "I can't believe Mike knows Stu the Sports Dude! Fungal!" —Seventh grader Jake Tripoli

- 🔊 "Fungal? Mike's video was so sick it was viral! It needs antibiotics!" —Big TOE, seventh grade

- 🔊 "Antibiotics are for bacterial infections, not viruses." —Ms. Cholley, school nurse

- 🔊 "I have a lot more time now that Peter Gronkowski's not sending me emails. Hey,

do you think Stu the Sports Dude could introduce me to Riley Reginald, the best pitcher in Poplar Pigeons history?"
—Mateo Medina, seventh grade

Clover's video drew mixed reactions:

- 🔊 "I'm not a big fart fan." —Larry Abrams, seventh grade

- 🔊 "Is farting presidential? Maybe, maybe not." —Seema Singh, seventh grade

- 🔊 "Clover's video had way better fart sounds than Mike's. She has my vote." —Alan Firenza, seventh grade

- 🔊 "I kept hearing the word 'period.' Was she talking about fifth period or second? I slept through them both." —Seamus Henry, seventh grade

- 🔊 "Did anyone else see monster trucks? Even I'm confused." —Holly Herman, seventh grade

◀) "I was in Spanish class? We watched a
video on verbs?" —Bea Salt, eighth grade

SUPPORT FOR ANITA TINKLE REMAINS STEADY.

◀) "Look, I think she can get the job done."
—Anonymous

POPLAR POLL
Mike: 46%
Clover: 45%
Anita Tinkle: 5%
Undecided: 4%

Peter Gronkowski Group Text

PETER:

Greetings,

I'd like to offer my services for your campaign.

Best,

Peter S. Gronkowski

CLOVER:

R U serious? 😵

PETER:

Yes. This is a legitimate offer, from a legitimate business professional.

RACHEL:

Where have I heard that one before . . . 🙃

PETER:

Hear me out. My relationship with Mike's campaign is in the past. Let's work together toward a more productive future.

RACHEL:
What's in it for you?

PETER:
Image rehab. My brand can't handle the stain of dirty money. Profits are already down. I want to help you AND make myself look good.

RACHEL:
At least you're honest.

CLOVER:
How can U help me?

PETER:
I can offer you my vast network of email addresses and cell phone numbers.

CLOVER:
I dunno . . .

RACHEL:
Me neither. But it's kind of fun,
watching him sweat.

PETER:
Hey, I can read that!

RACHEL:
Sorry. 😼

CLOVER:
No thx, Peter. 🖐

PETER:
WAIT. There's one more thing.

CLOVER:
???

PETER:
I can do makeup.

CLOVER:
U can??? 😻

PETER:

I'm licensed and everything. I'm a graduate of Rafael X's Online Course in Cosmetic Application. And I can bring my street team over to your campaign.

CLOVER:

Soooooo fungal. You're hired!

16

Clover

"Remember your promise, Clover!" Mom yelled on the way out.

"What promise?" Rachel asked as we left the house.

I sighed. "My parents made me promise not to get in trouble today," I said. "Violet heard about the farting sounds from Betsy and ratted me out. I *tried* to tell them the video just got messed up because of my subliminal messages. That didn't really help, though."

Peter was walking backward in front of me, trying to put makeup on my face on our way to school.

"Why did you put farts in your video?" Peter asked.

"Boys like farts, right?" I said.

Peter shrugged. "I find them unprofessional."

"Oh," I said. I felt kind of embarrassed. I'd assumed all boys thought farts were funny. But I guess all boys were different, just like all girls weren't the same, either.

When we got to school, Rachel pushed the front door open. "Why is it so quiet?" she asked.

Everyone in the lobby was crowded by the wall.

Mel Chang spotted us. She came over, holding up her phone like a recorder.

"Did you do it?" she asked me.

"Do what?" I said.

We walked to the wall where all the kids were clumped together.

I gasped when I saw what they were looking at.

Dr. Dana walked out of her office and straight over to me. "Clover O'Reilly, in my office," she said. "*Now.*"

I groaned. Not again.

What's New with
Mel Chang

— ⋛⋚ —

If It Trends, We're Friends.

THURSDAY

POSTER GATE!

Someone vandalized Mike's posters AND put up a new one. This poster perp means biz. Mean biz.

Witnesses reported red Xs through all the old posters. The new poster says: THE TRUTH ABOUT MIKE . . . THE UNUSUAL.

It makes totes damaging claims, some with photo evidence:

🔊 Mike does magic . . . and his only fans are in elem school.

🔊 Mike does puzzles.

🔊 Mike likes rom-coms.

- 🔊 Mike hates root beer. He drinks tea with his grandma.

- 🔊 Mike kisses baby dolls from Family and Consumer Services.

- 🔊 Mike doesn't have friends his own age, just acquaints.

- 🔊 Mike always does his homework.

- 🔊 Mike doesn't watch sports. He thought the Poplar Pigeons lived on a farm.

- 🔊 Mike has never seen his dad's show.

Mike's camp totes denies everything. "It's a smear campaign," said Mike's camp manager, Amelia Flem, prob re: the ink smeared all over the posters.

Who would do something so awf? If you have any info, please contact the Poplar Middle Crime-solvers.

17

Clover

Dr. Dana held up the THE TRUTH ABOUT MIKE . . . THE UNUSUAL poster.

"Let's talk," she said. "You're already on two strikes, Clover."

Rachel, Peter, and I sat on one side of her. Scott, Mike, and Amelia sat on the other.

"First of all, rom-coms are adorable," I said. "Why would that even be a bad thing? Obviously I didn't do it!"

"Of course you did!" Scott said. "It's sabotage! Who else would do this?"

"Peter would!" Amelia said. "He switched sides."

"That was business!" he said, glancing at Mike. "Not personal."

"I have no idea what happened," I told Dr. Dana. "I was semi-grounded last night. Plus, I would never do something so mean. Plus *plus*, that poster is totally not my artistic style. It's really sloppy, no offense to whoever made it."

"You scoff at the Integrity Contract!" said Scott. "And you make weird farting movies! Why should we believe you?"

Amelia looked furious. Her lips were pressed together so tight they almost disappeared.

"Rachel?" Dr. Dana said.

"She does have a vengeful side," Peter pointed out.

Rachel glared. "Hey! We're on the same team, Peter. And no, I didn't do it. I was at Amelia's house."

"You were?" I said.

She nodded.

"Oh," I said. Somehow that made everything worse.

"Peter?" Dr. Dana pressed.

"I spent last night watching makeup tutorials," he said. "I needed tips on doing makeup for girls. Plus, I'm Mike's mentor. At least I was. A mentor doesn't undermine a mentee."

"We'll have to work together to figure out who did this," Dr. Dana said. She looked at all of us but stared at me for a *particularly* long time.

"I'm keeping an eye on you," Scott said as we all stood up to leave. Then everyone on Mike's team except Mike glared at me.

Back in the hallway, everyone was staring at me and whispering. For the first time in my whole life, I didn't want to be at school.

"They think I did it," I said.

"No, some people think Peter did it," Rachel said helpfully.

Peter sniffed. "Is that how you treat a new team member?"

"But seriously," Rachel said. "Who would do this?"

"It could be anyone," Peter said.

We looked uneasily around the hall. Whoever it was, it was someone who wanted to hurt Mike. That was for sure.

I had to do something to clear my name.

WARTY MORTY'S TREATISE ON MAGIC

Copyright 1973

F *Is for "Forcing a Card"*

"Forcing a card" ain't some pushy fella shoving a queen of spades in your face.

Forcing a card is when you ask the spectator to choose a **card**, but you **force** them to pick one you already selected—and they think they picked it themselves. Far out, right?

A force is a way to control a spectator's choice, whether they're choosing a card, number, word, or letter. The magician who "forces" puts an idea into someone's head—no surgery required.

So how do you force a choice?

1. Rush your spectator into a decision.

2. Use subtle physical contact to guide them.

3. Flash the "target card" on the bottom of the pack during a trick, then move the card to the top of the pack.

Now here's an example of forcing a word. Let's say you include the words "head" and "ache" in your patter. So later when you read Johnny Audience's mind and try to guess the word he's thinking, there's a good chance he'll pick "headache." (Give the poor guy some aspirin, will ya?)

18

MIKE

We stood outside Dr. Dana's office after the meeting. There were just a few minutes left before homeroom.

I got lots of pats on the back. People kept telling me what a great guy I was and not to let it bother me. Some even said they'd definitely vote for me now.

If I had any idea Clover or Peter or Rachel would get blamed for what I did, I would never have done it. I didn't think that far ahead. I just wanted to tell the truth about myself. Clover's team didn't deserve this, not at all.

"I understand if you want to take away my badge," Scott said, looking me in the eye. "I let you down, man. And I've let down the service."

Amelia bit her lip. "I can't stop landing on the same question," she said. "Who would do this? It had to be Clover. Or Peter. But it doesn't really look like a professional job. Rachel was with me last night. Do you have any enemies, Mike?"

"None," I said. *Just myself*, I didn't say. "But it wasn't Clover. I mean, I don't think it could be. No way."

"Whoever it was, they said some pretty terrible things about you, man," Scott said. "It had to be a real enemy."

It made my stomach hurt that Scott would think the true things I said about myself were so terrible. Nothing I said was a lie. It was just the truth about me.

"Then who was it?" Amelia asked.

"I bet it was your girlfriend," Scott said. "Are you guys having problems, Mike? Is she jealous of your meteoric rise to fame?"

"Mike's girlfriend isn't real," Amelia reminded him.

"Maybe the leak came from inside the campaign," Scott said. "No one can be trusted."

The bell rang, cutting through awkward silence.

"What's our next move?" Scott asked. "What about Peter's opposition research file on Clover? You know, all the bad stuff about her. Do you still have it?"

Amelia nodded. "I know we'll look weak if we don't do something. But I don't want to be negative about Clover if we don't have to. We're not sure she did anything. That's not the kind of leader you want to be. Right, Mike?"

I shook my head.

"Okay then," said Scott. "In the meantime, I'll keep my eyes on Mike around the clock. And on Clover, too. I'm not sure how I'll do that with only two eyes, but I'll figure it out. Maybe I'll tap her phone."

"How do you tap a phone?" I asked.

"Gently," Scott said.

My heart thudded. I had to do something to clear Clover's name.

What's New with
Mel Chang

———— ⁊ ⁋ ————

If It Trends, We're Friends.

ANOTHER THURSDAY POST!

EVEN MORE BREAKING, SHATTERED NEWS! ARE YOU SERIOUS, MEL?!

Yep.

In response to the SCANDALOUS poster THE TRUTH ABOUT MIKE . . . THE UNUSUAL, an ANON SOURCE has sent me a text titled THE TRUTH ABOUT CLOVER . . . O'REILLY.

THE SCOOP:

🔊 Clover is brave—she isn't afraid to say what she thinks.

🔊 Clover smells like pickles (that's good).

🔊 Clover is generous—she shares ideas and art supplies.

🔊 Clover would be a great leader.

Is Clover's team trying to plant positive stories in the press to save face? You decide.

Clover is holding a press conference TODAY, AFTER SCHOOL, BY THE TREE STUMP (THE CROOKED ONE BY THE FLAGPOLE) to address the scandal.

In the interest of fair journalism, I'm printing the following student theory re: who destroyed Mike's posters. I think you'll agree it's ridic:

🔊 "It was Mike. He did it himself." —Holly Herman, seventh grade

Others worried about how the election might be affecting a Poplar Middle VIP.

"Mel," said Katie Lepore, eighth grade, "take a long, hard look at yourself. It's a seventh-grade election. Seventh grade. You're an eighth grader now. Do something else. Adopt a pet. Paint your nails."

PLUS! Mel Chang's EXCLUSIVE INTER-VIEW with "Mikayla," who claims to be Mike's mystery girlfriend. "Relationships are hard," says Mikayla. "They're even harder when you're dating the future president."

19

Clover

The crowd around the tree stump was buzzing before my press conference.

"Where's Peter?" I asked.

"Running late," Rachel said, reading a text on her phone. "He's picking up plants from Poplar Elementary."

"Plants?" I asked. "This is no time to run errands! And anyway, the press conference is outside. We don't need any."

Rachel squinted at something barreling down the sidewalk. "There he is."

Peter was pulling a wagon carrying his brother Daniel, Susie Lorenzo, and Gabby Jonas.

When he got to us, he patted his forehead with a white handkerchief that had his initials on it.

"Apologies for the delay," Peter said. "I had to pick up the street team."

"Where are the plants?" I asked.

"Here," he said, gesturing to the kids in the wagon. "Plants sit in the audience and ask questions to make you look good."

"Why do Susie and Gabby look like melted clowns?" Rachel asked.

Peter shook his head. "I let them do each other's makeup on the way over," he said. "The ride got bumpy. Professional error on my part."

Daniel hopped out of the wagon and did a jig. He was wearing a leprechaun costume. "I'm not a plant," he said. "I'm a four-leaf clover!"

"It was Career Day at school," Peter said, like that explained anything. "I'll set them up in the audience. And don't worry, they know what to say."

Rachel stood on top of the tree stump and cleared her throat. "Thank you all for coming out to today's press conference," she said. "Clover will take *respectful* questions from the audience. Clover?"

I took the stage—um, stump. "Thanks for coming out to hear my side of the story," I said. "I didn't mess up Mike's posters. Period."

Some people in the audience snickered.

"But I totally want to help Mike figure out who did it," I said. "Oh, and I'd like to know who glued pickle chips to my posters. That was really mean. Thank you."

Rachel scanned the crowd and pointed. "First question goes to . . . Mel Chang."

Mel stood up. She always goes first.

"For the rec, did you destroy Mike's posters and make the new, really bad one?" Mel asked.

"As I said, absolutely not."

"Then who did it?" she asked.

Rachel stood up. "Clover doesn't want to accuse anybody," she said. "We're just trying to get the facts."

"Can you describe your relash with known troublemaker Thalia Jung?" Mel pressed.

"Relash?"

"Relationship!" Peter called from the crowd.

"Uh, I know her?" I said.

The crowd murmured.

"Can you also confirm the info revealed in THE TRUTH ABOUT CLOVER . . . O'REILLY?" Mel asked.

"What info?"

"The info describes you as generous. Says you smell good. That you'd be a great leader."

"Wow!" I said. "Yeah, smelling good is extremely important to me. I take a lot of showers. The rest is true, too!"

Seema Singh raised her hand. She wasn't wearing her rubber band bracelets. "So you agree with what the person said?" she asked.

I shrugged. "Sure."

"Does that make you conceited?" Seema asked.

"I don't think so," I said.

The crowd murmured louder.

Daniel raised his hand. He was sitting on a stack of books. I nodded.

"Do you have fruit snacks?" he asked.

"No?" I said.

Peter whispered something in Daniel's ear.

"Is it true you want girl power?" Daniel asked.

"Yes!" I said. "Thank you for your great question."

"No fair! I want girl power, too," Daniel said. "*Now!*" He threw himself on the ground and started wailing.

Peter whisked Daniel out of the audience, placing him back in the wagon with a packet of fruit snacks.

"Moving on," said Rachel. "Seamus?"

"What's your position on homework reform?" he asked me. "Are you going to get rid of it like Mike?"

"I don't like homework," I said. "But I don't think teachers are going to just get rid of it. That doesn't make sense."

"Disappointing," said Seamus, yawning. "And now, a follow-up question. Do you know Stu the Sports Dude?"

"Mike's dad?" I asked. "He's my neighbor."

"Can you get me tickets to see a live taping of a Stu the Sports Dude show?" Seamus asked.

"Probably . . . not?" I said.

The audience buzzed. Seamus clucked his tongue and shook his head.

Gabby Jonas raised her hand.

"Watch this move," she said. She got a running start and did a roundhouse kick in the air.

"Huh?"

Peter steered Gabby out of the press conference and set her beside Daniel in the wagon.

Mel raised her hand again.

"Breaking news," she said. "I just received a list of claims against you from an anon source. Can you confirm or deny?"

She started reading before I could say anything. "You don't always wash your hands after you go to the bathroom," she said. "You pull belly button lint out of your stomach and smell it. You eat ketchup with a spoon. You bite your toenails." She looked at Rachel. "Should I go on?"

"Clover denies all these claims," Rachel said.

"Well, not all of them," I said.

"It also says you think boys are annoying," Mel said.

"Hey!" said Brayden Monk.

"That's so uncool it's burning hot," said Big TOE.

"Not all boys," I said.

"But some!" said Alan Firenza.

The crowd got louder.

Susie raised her hand.

I nodded, hoping her planned question would save me.

"Do you think my makeup is designive?" Susie asked.

"It's kind of . . . smeared," I said.

"I'll fix it!" Gabby yelled, waving makeup brushes from the wagon. Peter stood in her path so she couldn't get out.

"Oh! What's your plan for increasing student involvement in the political process?" Susie asked.

Peter looked shocked. Rachel beamed.

"When I'm president, I want everyone to have a

say in their government!" I said. "Great question!"

"I have another great question!" said Susie. "Is your mom having a baby?"

I gasped. "What? Who told you that?"

Susie shrugged. "Not telling."

"I got scooped by a second grader?" Mel said. She pointed her phone toward me. "Is it true?"

Hot tears spilled down my face. All these questions and my family's secret coming out were too much to deal with all at once.

I nodded.

"This press conference is over," Rachel said.

As the crowd cleared out, Rachel put her arm around my shoulder.

"That was rough," she said. "Is your mom really pregnant? Why didn't you tell me?"

"She said not to tell anyone yet," I said. "I'm sorry."

"That's okay," she said.

"I felt like I was on trial," I said through my sniffles. "And I didn't do anything wrong. Who sent Mel all that bad stuff about me? And how did Susie find out about my mom?"

Peter walked up beside us. "Maybe it was Amelia," he said.

"What do you mean?"

"She'd have access to your opposition research file," Peter said. "I left it with Mike's campaign. Some of the stuff Mel said is what I heard at your pool party."

"Seriously?" I said. "Don't expect me to invite you to anything ever again!"

Peter waved his hand. "I was doing my job," he said. "Anyway, Amelia volunteers for your mom's campaign, right? She must have found out your mom was pregnant and leaked it to the press."

"Amelia wouldn't do that," Rachel said.

"You barely know her," I said. "Maybe she wants to destroy me!"

"She just wants to be your friend," said Rachel.

"Whose side are you on?"

Rachel shook her head. "There aren't sides. She's not your enemy."

I wiped away my tears. "Stop defending her," I said. "If she's doing opposition research on me, I'm doing some on her."

What's New with
Mel Chang

—— ⸙ ——

If It Trends, We're Friends.

MY THIRD THURSDAY POST— A "WHAT'S NEW WITH MEL CHANG" RECORD!

Student support increases for Mike.

- ◄) "SMELLING your BELLY BUTTON LINT is not presidential. GAG." —Seema Singh, seventh grader and former Clover supporter

- ◄) "Even if Clover didn't do it, she probably released the Clover O'Reilly file, which was all just nice stuff about her. And even if she didn't release that stuff, she agreed with it. That's conceited . . . right?" —Hannah Greer, seventh grade

🔊 "My dad says girls are too emotional to be president. And Clover cried. You do the math." —Brayden Monk (ED note: Brayden is currently failing math.)

POPLAR POLL

🔊 55% of students who attended Clover's press conf found the candidate to be "too defensive."

🔊 65% of students ID'd Clover as a "crybaby," with only 35% calling her a "leader."

Others disliked the tone of the press conf:

🔊 "Dude, some of those questions were so mean they gave ME a wedgie." —Big TOE, seventh grader

🔊 "Why is everybody jumping on Clover? Here's my question: Why is there a picture of Mike kissing a baby doll?" —Thalia Jung, seventh grade

Some voters are just ready for election season to end:

- ◀) "Am I SERIOUSLY getting emails from Peter again?" asked seventh grader Mateo Medina. "And why are the wagon children back? That's it. I'm calling a lawyer."

- ◀) "Mel, this is an intervention," read an unsigned folded-up note passed in third period. "Please. Stop. Reporting. On. Seventh. Graders."

BONUS FEATURE! Nurse Cholley shares Facts about Fungus. "All I'm hearing is fungal this, fungal that. You kids need to start wearing clean socks."

WARTY MORTY'S
TREATISE ON MAGIC

Copyright 1973

P *Is for "Parlor Magic"*

Parlor magic, also called platform magic, falls between close-up magic (where the magician performs so close you can smell his garlic breath) and stage magic (a big, fancy show where the audience sits too far away to smell any garlic breath. Lucky audience!). "Parlor" is an old word for living room.

Lots of folks know the term "**parlor tricks**." They use it in a negative way, like when a salesman or politician lies or tries to pull one over on you.

But parlor magic is near and dear to Warty Morty's heart. Take the **sand frame**, a parlor magic illusion where a photo, card, or other flat item mysteriously appears in an empty picture frame.

Professor J. Hartford Armstrong, a successful black magician, brought black history into his sand frame routine. First he'd show the audience an empty picture frame. Then he'd pass around a picture of Frederick Douglass, an abolitionist, orator, and statesman. Somewhere along the way, the picture of Frederick Douglass would appear in the frame!

FUN FACT-O-RAMA

After Professor Armstrong died, his daughter Ellen took over his stage show. Ellen also cracked up crowds with **chalk talk**, a technique where she'd draw funny cartoons for the audience based on their suggestions. Ellen Armstrong was likely the only black woman magician of her time to run an independent magic touring show in the United States.

20

MIKE

"How's the campaign going?" Granberry asked me. We were drinking chamomile tea and putting together an optical illusion puzzle. The picture on the box could be either two faces or one, depending on how you looked at it.

"The election is tomorrow," I said. I was getting pretty good at not answering questions.

"You didn't answer my question," she said. Well, maybe I wasn't that good. She laughed. "You're turning into a politician. Don't be a politician. Be a leader."

"What's the difference?" I asked.

"A leader makes decisions based on what they feel," she said. "A politician just goes along with what people want to get votes."

I thought about firing Peter and letting Clover take the fall for my messed-up posters. I didn't want to be a politician, but along the way, I'd turned into one.

"Haven't seen you do many tricks in a while," Granberry said, sorting through a pile of light blue puzzle pieces.

I shrugged. I'd been doing plenty of tricks, but none of them were magic.

"Magic is like politics," she said. "A whole lot of tricks." She wiggled a puzzle piece into one of the faces, but it didn't quite fit. "It's political in other ways, too."

"What ways?" I asked.

"For instance," she said. "Have you ever seen a woman do a magic trick?"

"Huh?" I asked. "Yeah, you."

"Other than me," she said.

I thought really hard. "No," I said.

"But woman magicians exist, right?" she said. "Even if you don't see them?"

I nodded.

"That's politics," she said. "The fight to be seen and heard."

She stirred her tea.

"Imagine this," she said. "You're a woman in magic, so right there you're invisible. And you're also black in a field with few black magicians. I didn't really have a community."

Granberry held up the puzzle box, squinting hard at the picture. She shook her head and set it down.

"You know how I taught you about magic?" Granberry asked. I nodded. "Nobody ever taught me. Especially nobody who looked like me. So I taught myself. I learned from books. My hero was Ellen Armstrong."

I nodded. Granberry talked about her a lot.

"She was a pioneer," Granberry said. "I read everything I could about her. But there wasn't a whole lot to read, just a few articles here and there. But they proved she was real, and that was enough for me.

"When I was a teenager, I met Granbobby. He was doing some coin magic after church. I showed him a few tricks, and he showed me a few of his. I found my kindred spirit in magic. Eventually, we took our show on the road."

I'd always thought Granberry was just Granbobby's assistant.

"We booked mostly churches and school functions," she said. "Those were the places we felt welcome. I made most of our props. I sewed the costumes, played the music, developed our act. I even wrote a book."

"Whoa," I said. "What book?"

She nodded at the end table. "That one. *Warty Morty's Treatise on Magic*."

I shook my head. "Wait," I said. "*You* wrote that? But Granbobby was Warty Morty."

She laughed. "They call it ghostwriting," she said. "And that's how it felt. Like invisible work."

"Why did Granbobby do that?" I asked. "That's not fair."

"He didn't," she said. "I wanted him to take credit. It was better for our career to use his name. He was the headliner. And frankly, at that point, I was used to being behind the scenes. I didn't know if I was ready to come out from behind the curtain, as they say."

I picked the book off the end table and opened it.

"Read the dedication message," she said, smiling.

It said, "To the invisible people: show yourselves. Be seen."

I swallowed.

"Here's the truth," she said. "Every time I see that book, it hurts. I should have put my name on there. It seems important now."

She wiggled another puzzle piece into the face. This time, it fit.

———○———

That night, I couldn't stop thinking about Granberry. She'd dedicated her book to invisible people like me. But even though I was "showing myself" by running for president, the real me was still hiding. My lying wasn't just bad. It disrespected Granberry.

The whole time I was thinking, I kept getting texts from my team.

AMELIA:
Did you memorize your speech yet?

SCOTT:
Hey, man, I'm outside your house. No one is trying to get in. Just thought you'd like to know. 😎

AMELIA:
Did you see Mel's polls? You're on top! You're so close to winning! 😁

I looked at the screenshot in Amelia's text. It was Mel's poll. I cringed reading all the bad stuff people said about Clover.

Like Amelia said, I was so close to winning. And that's even after I tried to sabotage everything.

I couldn't even screw up my campaign right.

There was only one thing left to do. I had to drop out of the race.

21

Clover

If Amelia Flem was going to spill my family's secrets, I would spill hers.

I just had to find out what they were. And there was one place everyone kept their secrets: on the internet.

Rachel had stormed off after the press conference, so I walked home alone. All the way, I kept thinking about Amelia spying on me. She sat at our dinner table, in my seat. She was probably collecting secrets right then and betraying my mom the whole time. Maybe she was really working for Rocket Shipley!

I felt a little like Holly Herman, but as Rachel says, a stopped clock is right twice a day.

Mom was checking her phone when I came into the kitchen. "Clover!" she said. "So the cat's out of

★ 223 ★

the bag. I'm getting congratulation texts on the pregnancy."

"I know!" I said. "It's going around school. And I think I know who did it."

"Oh, I know who did it," Mom said.

"You do?" I asked. "Devious, right? Can you believe her?"

"Sure," Mom said. "I mean, Daisy's only four. I shouldn't have expected her to keep a secret."

"Huh?" I asked. "Daisy?"

Daisy ran into the kitchen. "I only told my whole preschool class!" she said. "Can I have a lollipop?"

Mom reached into the pantry for the bag of lollipops. "In a way, it's a relief," she said. "I was only hiding it because I thought people would judge me. You know, if a woman is pregnant, she can't do the job, it's an inconvenience." She waved her hand. "Blah, blah, blah."

Daisy snatched a mango lollipop and ran off.

"The worst part is, I was repeating that nonsense to you girls," Mom said. "And none of it's true. It's not an inconvenience. But the more I kept quiet about the pregnancy, the more I started feeling . . . inconvenient. So I'm glad it's out there."

I grabbed a raspberry lollipop. Okay, so Amelia

Flem didn't spill the beans about Mom. But what about that other stuff? Like eating ketchup off my toenails, or whatever Mel said.

That could have been Daisy, too, I guess. Or even Dahlia. But what if it wasn't?

I went upstairs and searched "Amelia Flem" on my computer. She had an InstaVid account with lots of pictures and videos, all titled "My First Day of School."

Why were there so many?

I clicked on the latest picture, which was dated last Monday, our first day of school. It was a selfie of Amelia with a huge grin on her face. I'd never seen her smile like that before.

The caption said:

It's my thirteenth first day of school! You know how on the first day you feel scared and hopeful and excited and anxious? I've felt that, like, a lot more than most people. It's hard because I don't want to be pushy, but at the same time, you have to work hard to make friends. If I don't work hard, I won't have any.

I swallowed. I'd lived here all my life. I didn't know what it was like being the new kid and having to start over, over and over again. I kept reading.

I met a girl named Rachel over the summer. I feel like we could be real friends, not just until I move friends.

Under the caption was a comment from Amelia:

UPDATE: It was an A-minus day! Rachel invited me to walk to school with her! And I got to meet her best friend, Clover! She's really friendly and good at art. When I get nervous I talk a lot. I hope I didn't embarrass myself.

That was the last entry.

My face felt hot. I remembered the first day of school. Amelia had asked me so many questions about myself, and honestly, I thought she was pretty annoying. But I had my own problems. I was sad and mad that I wasn't getting my own room, and I wanted to tell Rachel all about it, and I couldn't. So even though Amelia said I was friendly, I wasn't as nice to her as I could have been.

And I was jealous. Jealous that Rachel made a new friend, a friend she had other stuff in common with. Stuff she didn't have in common with me. It made me scared there wasn't room for me anymore.

Amelia didn't have to be my best friend, but she didn't have to be my enemy. I never gave her a chance to be anything in between. And there *was* something in between. I could have just said hi in the hallway or asked her to sit with us at lunch, just once. Instead, I pushed her away and tried to tear her down so Rachel would like me better. I was a girl power hypocrite.

I added a comment under Amelia's picture: "Welcome to Poplar Middle School!" I typed. "I can't wait to get to know you better."

Maybe that was real girl power, being a friend to someone new and helping her through a tough time. There could be room for everyone.

I checked the clock. I still had to write my speech for tomorrow. Usually Rachel writes my speeches, but I was pretty sure she wouldn't be in the mood after our fight.

Besides, I needed to do it myself, without help. Without a filter.

What's New with
Mel Chang

——— ⅔ ⅔ ———

If It Trends, We're Friends.

FRIDAY

SPESH ENDORSEMENT EDITION

All the big profesh publications endorse a candidate. So without further ado, here's my eval of the seventh-grade pres campaigns.

MERCH

Mike: Stickers
Clover: Rubber bracelets

At first I thought Clover's rubber bracelets were five-star hot. They were all diff colors, so you could wear them with lots of outfits.

And voters stated that Mike's stickers were

poor quality, complaining they lost their stickiness in humid places like the gym and cafeteria.

But Mike's stickers are trending over Clover's bracelets, because more peeps are wearing them.

Round 1: Slight edge to Mike.

REFRESH

Mike: Gave out root beer at the Candidate Luncheon. Some voters complained it was generic but admitted "it tasted the same." Also, great tie-in with Peter's Pie-Crust Cookies.

Clover: Skipped Candidate Luncheon; zero root beer or other snacks

Round 2: Mike, easily.

VIP ENDORSEMENTS

Mike: Endorsed by Stu the Sports Dude

Clover: Endorsed by . . . nobody? Word

on Poplar Lane is that her own campaign manager is mad at her.

Round 3: Mike, by a landslide.

VERDICT: Five stars to Mike for President.

★ ★ ★ ★ ★

(ED. NOTE: I reached out to stylist Rafael X to get his pick for Most Stylish Candidate. As of press time, he had not replied to my InstaVid comment.)

22

Clover

Over the treetops and 'round the bend,
Poplar Middle School is a friend till the end.
It's our school spirit that sets us apart,
A whole lot of joy and a whole lot of . . . HEART!

I hardly even heard the FART echo. My hands were shaking with excitement.

"Thank you," Dr. Dana told the Poplar Middle School Pops after they finished playing. "We'll start with our first candidate for seventh-grade class president. Ms. O'Reilly, please take the stage."

"Thank you, Dr. Dana," I said. "And hello, Poplar Middle School!"

I unzipped my gold glitter hoodie. Underneath was a T-shirt I'd made with a giant glitter-cat ear on it.

"I think a president should be a good listener," I

said, pointing to my glitter ear. "And let's be honest, I'm not the best. I get really bad earwax clogs, but it's more than that. My dad says I don't have a filter. I need to work on that, because I've messed up and hurt people."

I took off my ear shirt, my shout-out to Daisy. There was another shirt underneath that said: #LOUD.

"Ms. O'Reilly, are we through with the disrobing?" Dr. Dana said.

"Last one!" I said. "The weird thing about running for president is that you're not supposed to talk about how you really feel. You're supposed to hide your message. You're supposed to say what gets votes.

"Girls do that, too. Not always to get votes. But they think they have to act a certain way to get people to like them. People tell girls to smile even if they're mad or sad or upset. That's hiding a message. And we think we can't disagree or have any bad feelings, because that's mean. So we keep our real feelings hidden. And the weird thing is, if we're honest about how we feel, we're called mean *again*! But they're just feelings. Boys have them, too. Am I rambling?"

"Yes!" shouted someone in the audience.

"Thank you for your honesty!" I said. "Girl power isn't just a slogan. It's an action. It's saying what you

mean, and meaning what you say, and having different opinions, and being okay with that. And seeing
that you have more friends than enemies. You might
have more in common with someone than you think."

I took a deep breath.

"In summary, I don't want to be mean, but I also
don't want to hide my message. So here it is: I don't
want to be president."

The audience gasped.

"Is this is a joke?" asked Dr. Dana.

"Nope," I said. "I'm dropping out. Being loud can
cause problems, but it's also my strength. I'm not giving that up."

For a second no one said anything. Then a bunch
of people started cheering. Thalia Jung even stood
up, starting a standing ovation in her section.

I'd never felt so proud in my whole life.

I scanned the crowd. I knew Rachel was probably
still kind of mad, but when I found her, she gave me
a thumbs-up.

Amelia stood in a corner by the EXIT sign. It was
kind of hard to see with the stage lights in my face,
but I'm pretty sure she was wearing the glitter-cat
apology necklace I put in her locker this morning.
And she was definitely smiling.

WARTY MORTY'S TREATISE ON MAGIC

V *Is for* "*VANISHING*"

In 1849, a man named Henry "Box" Brown delivered himself from slavery to freedom in—you guessed it—a box. He lived the rest of his life a free man and a civil rights activist. In later years, Henry performed as a professional magician, using the same box that set him free in his act.

A true escape artist.

In magic parlance, **vanishing** is the opposite of **production**, when the magician produces something from nothing.

Most magicians think vanishing is as easy as disappearing in a puff of smoke. To which I say, "Ha!" (or I might cough, as smoke doesn't agree with my lungs). Sadly, or perhaps fortunately, most magicians aren't roaming the earth with smoke bombs in their pockets.

Most vanishings involve one simple trick: mirrors.

There's this gent—you may have heard of him—named Harry Houdini. He made an elephant disappear. Did he snap his fingers and send the monstrous beast into the ether?

Nope. He used mirrors.

It's a matter of physics. Magicians have many tools in their bag of tricks to misdirect an audience: sleight of hand, a clever turn of phrase, distracting movements. But fooling the eye, the optical illusion, involves the simple principles of mirrors, angles, and light.

My point? It's rather sharp, thank you for asking. Oh, the other point? A magician never really vanishes.

23

MIKE

I won.

It was kind of a whirlwind after Clover's speech. The crowd went wild. Then Dr. Dana blew a whistle and announced we wouldn't need to vote, because I won by default. And I didn't feel like I could drop out after Clover did, because then there wouldn't be any president at all. So I took a bow. Everybody clapped.

And now all I wanted was to disappear.

That night, Dad ordered three extra-large pizzas with my favorite toppings: olives and onions. Mom even called us on SkyTime. She was eating pizza on the soccer field so she could feel like she was there.

"Presidential pizza tastes good!" she said. She'd told all the players and coaches and everything. Her smile was so proud it made my heart hurt.

Granberry made pecan pie. From scratch.

"A Strange family recipe," she said. "I haven't made one in years, but I figured this was cause for a real celebration! You did good, Mike."

I took a bite. It was the best pie I'd ever had. I didn't deserve it.

"May I please be excused?" I asked.

"That bad, huh?" Granberry said.

"No, it's great," I said. "I'll be right back."

I went to my room, plopped down on my bed, and stared at the ceiling. Houdini could break locks, escape from underwater boxes, and wiggle his way out of straitjackets. But I'm not sure even he could get out of the mess I'd made.

The doorbell rang. I waited. A few seconds later, someone knocked on my door.

"It's Amelia!" Dad called. "I asked her to come in for some pizza."

I jumped up. I hadn't seen her since Dr. Dana said I was the winner. She probably wanted to talk about strategy. Now that I was president, I had to actually do presidential stuff. I needed her more than ever.

But when I stepped out on the porch, Amelia wasn't

smiling. She didn't wiggle or squeal or congratulate me. In fact, she looked ready to strangle me.

"I'm going to ask you one question," she said. "And I want you to be honest. For once."

For once? I got prickles on my arms.

"Okay," I said.

"Did you mess up your posters?"

"What?"

"Are you," she said slowly, "the one. Who messed up. Your posters. Because I think you are."

"Yes," I said. I felt totally exposed, like my tricks were spilling out of my pocket, an avalanche of secrets, all over the floor.

"I thought so," she said.

"How did you know?"

"I mean, I thought about it for hours. Hours! But I couldn't imagine anyone who would actually take the time to do all of that. And then I remembered the Xs all over your posters. Like the Xs you drew on the posters at Clover's party. So I knew you did it. But why did you do it?"

"I . . . don't know."

"Could you try to think of an answer?" she asked.

"It's just . . . I never really wanted to be president," I said. "I only ran so I could write an essay to get into magic camp. And to make my dad think I was cool."

"I want you to know something," she said. "You wasted a whole lot of my time. I was trying to build your campaign while you were destroying it."

I never thought about it that way, that my actions to protect myself could hurt someone else.

"I'm sorry," I said.

"I'm glad you're sorry," she said. "Because I feel used. I was trying to make friends. And I thought we were becoming friends. And then I find out you betrayed me. And that really, really hurt. And normally I wouldn't say anything. But because you're my friend, or I thought you were, I want you to hear the truth."

Then I started to feel mad. "Hey, you say I'm your friend, but you wanted me to be a different person!" I said. "You didn't want me to be myself."

She looked down. "Maybe you're right. I was just trying to go with what worked. I was trying to help us both fit in."

"I didn't ask for your help."

"Yes, you did," she said quietly.

She was right. We both were. We were both wrong, too.

The silence felt heavy.

"What do we do now?" I asked. "Because I really don't want to be president."

"You can resign."

"But then . . . it's over," I said. And it hit me. It would be over. As much as the election was making me miserable, it made me kind of special. I was afraid to go back to being myself.

"You're right," she said. "Then it's over. Isn't that a relief? It is for me. I'm just done with trying so hard," she said. "Trying to figure people out, thinking I have to be a certain way to make friends. And the truth is, it never worked anyway! So I'm going to . . . retire." She said "retire" slowly, like she was pronouncing a new word in a different language. "At least for today. I love being a wonk. But I think people are more like art than science. They're unpredictable. They're not really categories or formulas, no matter what they look like on the outside. And that's good."

"But I don't know what to do," I said. I didn't want to beg, but I was pretty close to getting down on my knees.

"I say this as your friend," Amelia said. "And it's my last piece of advice. For today, at least."

"What is it?"

"I'm glad you asked," she said. She grabbed me by my shoulders. "Figure it out." She smiled.

And then she walked away.

24

Clover

I walked home after school. Even though I was super proud of myself, my whole body felt achy, like I'd just been through the non-delicate cycle of the washing machine.

I needed waffles. With extra syrup.

I wasn't expecting to walk into a kitchen full of pink balloons.

"Clover, we have big news!" Dad said.

He shoved a black-and-white picture in my face. It was a blob with a sort-of baby face.

"It's a girl!" Mom said.

"Wow," I choked out. My throat was scratchy from yelling my speech.

"Six girls," Dad said, beaming. "Six! Isn't that fun?"

"Fun?" I said. "Can I tell you something not fun? I dropped out of the election."

Mom's smile faded. "Oh, honey. Why?"

"Because," I said. It wasn't like me to hide stuff, but I also didn't feel like spilling my guts to my parents just then.

Dad gave me a hug. "We have a whole weekend ahead of us," he said. "And now that you have more free time, you can give us some design advice for the nursery."

"No!" I said, pulling away from him. "I want my own room, like you promised. You're so glad it's 'out in the open' that you're having another kid. What about the kids you have now? Don't you care about them?"

Daisy started crying, and then Juniper.

"I *hate* the baby!" Dahlia yelled.

She ran out of the room in tears.

"Dahlia!" Dad yelled after her. "Come back right now."

"You know what?" I said. "I kind of hate the baby, too. You just want to hum and have a new kid rather than deal with the kids you already have. What's wrong with us? What's wrong with what you have?"

I bolted from the room before Dad could say anything.

———◆———

I didn't hate the baby. Not really. I can't say I *loved* the baby, because I didn't know it—her—yet. Something was wrong. But the baby wasn't the problem.

When I walked into my room, Violet was coloring with Dahlia. Adrenaline swished through my veins.

"Don't you have your own room?" I asked Violet.

Violet looked up at me. Her three different colors of eyeliner were wet and all smudged together. It was kind of beautiful and kind of sad at the same time.

"The crayons are in here," she said. "And Dahlia wants to color."

I wanted to say more mean things to Violet, like ask her why she only wanted to see us when it was convenient for her.

But Dahlia wasn't crying anymore. She was drawing hearts and making a card that said, "I'm sorry" at the top. And I didn't want to make her sad again.

"I'm sorry," Dahlia told me. "I'm sorry for hurting the baby."

"You didn't hurt the baby," I said.

"Do you think Mom and Dad will forget us?" Dahlia said.

I felt a pit expanding in my stomach. Dahlia and I were in the middle-child netherworld, that confusing zone where you wonder how much you really matter.

Violet helped Dahlia cut out a heart.

"Nope," Violet told her. "And even if they do, we have each other. The Sister Alliance."

Then Violet smiled at me. She actually smiled. She wasn't in the middle like Dahlia and me, but we were all sisters. Together.

———•———

Later Mom walked in. She looked like she'd been crying.

"I don't hate the baby," I told her.

"Me neither," said Dahlia.

"I'm dropping out of the election," Mom said.

"What? Why?"

"I can handle the politics part," Mom said. "It's just a game, and I know the rules. What I can't handle is seeing you guys hurting. You need me."

I wanted to tell Mom we didn't need her, but that wasn't true.

"And the new baby needs me, too," Mom said.

"Then why do you want another kid?" I asked. "I know that wasn't a filter question. But why?"

She looked at me. "Because of the love we have for you. It's infinite. And we wanted to create more of it."

"But you can't create time," Violet said. "Or money. Or bedrooms. Those are finite resources. And the truth is, you take all that away from us when you have another kid."

Violet sounded really smart. Maybe she was doing extra studying now that she had her own room.

"Yeah!" I said, even though I wasn't totally sure what Violet meant. "Why didn't you ask us first?"

"This might be hard to hear," Mom said. "But a family is not a democracy. The parents are in charge. We make the rules."

"But are we nothing?" I asked.

"You're not nothing," Dad said in the doorway.

"Then you should have asked us first."

"Maybe you're right," Mom said. "But there's a baby coming. And we have to figure out how to welcome her into our lives. Can you do that?"

"As long as you don't forget us," I said.

Mom smiled. "I could never forget you," she said.

———◦———

The next morning I had a great idea.

"I have a great idea," I told Mom.

"What's that?" she asked.

"You haven't dropped out of the election yet, right?"

"Not yet. I will on Monday."

"Well, don't."

"Clover, I—"

"Do you want to be on the school board?"

"Part of me does, yes. Very much so. But I don't want our family under attack. All these negative ads and rumors and how it's affecting you girls—it's not worth it."

"What if your family fights *with* you?" I asked. "Strength in numbers! I mean, our family *is* pretty huge."

She smiled a little.

"Okay," I said. "I get that a family is not a democracy all the time. I don't like it, but I kind of get it. We didn't get to vote on you having a baby. But maybe we, our family, can vote on you staying in the election."

Mom's smile got bigger. "Really?"

"Yes," I said. "But be prepared for anything. Elections are always surprising."

———o———

That night we held our family election. The question at the top of the ballot was "Should Mom run for school board?"

We even had 100 percent voter turnout. Everyone showed up, even baby Juniper (she kind of had to because she was attached to Dad's hip). Mom voted, too. Violet even set up an election day face-painting station.

I built a voting booth by hanging baby blackout curtains around Daisy's coloring desk. One at a time, each member of the O'Reilly household went into the booth to cast their votes.

"How do we know what Juniper wants to vote for?" Dahlia asked.

I thought hard. "She copies everything Daisy does. Daisy, will you cast Juniper's vote?"

Daisy nodded.

After dinner, I counted the votes.

"We have the results of the election," I said dramatically. "In a unanimous decision, the O'Reilly family has decided that Mom will keep running for school board!"

"Beat the Rocket Ship!" said Dahlia.

"Thank you," Mom said, her voice shaking just a little.

"And we know you can't do it alone," I said. "So Violet and I are prepared to swap older-sister babysitting duties."

"And I'll help do cooking," Daisy said.

"No!" said Dahlia. "I don't want fart casserole."

Dad bent over laughing. When he stood up, he had tears streaming down his face.

"Dad, I didn't know you had tears!" Dahlia said. She handed Mom and Dad a card with six hearts on it. One for each kid, including the new baby.

FROM

WARTY MORTY'S TREATISE ON MAGIC

Copyright 1973

R *Is for "RECOVERY"*

There are some certainties in life. Death. Taxes. Chicken-pox. And exposure.

Nothing indecent, of course. I'm talking about bungling a trick.

Take Fetaque Sanders, the famous black comedy magician. In 1933, during his very first professional stage appearance, he attempted a trick called Cutting a Girl in Two with Ropes. He got a volunteer from the audience and fastened two pieces of rope around her waist. He pulled at one of the ropes. Neither rope would budge. Did he run offstage? No! He said, "Suppose we try another trick."

And did the audience boo? No! They laughed (I bet the volunteer was pretty happy about it, too). The rest of his show went off without a hitch. In fact, the manager of the theater offered him a two-week booking.

Even the greatest magicians will fail. Props break. You flash a card or drop a coin.

There's only one thing to do: recover.

The way Ol' Morty sees it, there are three possible recoveries:

1. Keep going. Most likely no one noticed.

2. Create a new ending—some other magical outcome to end on a happy note. Experienced magicians have what's called an "out." That's when they expect to fail, so they've got another trick ready to go in their back (or side!) pocket. Roll with the punches, and hopefully you won't be the one getting punched.

3. Admit you made a mistake. Laugh it off. An audience can be pretty forgiving, so long as you wow 'em with your next trick. Some magicians might wag their fingers and say, "MORTY, YOU FOOL, YOU SHOULD NEVER ADMIT DEFEAT!" But sometimes it's the only way out. And life, as they say, goes on.

25

MIKE

I had to break the news to my family.

"Thank you all for coming to my Family Luncheon," I said. "Please help yourself to, uh, pickles. And milk. And M&M's." I'm a comedy magician, not a chef.

"I guess we have to do what the president says," Dad said, grinning. He dug into the spread.

I took a deep breath and stood up.

"I'm not going to be president anymore," I said. "I'm resigning on Monday."

They stopped eating.

"Mike," Dad said.

"Why?" Granberry asked. "You can't just resign."

I felt a little dizzy. I wanted to sit down, or hide, or take back my words, but it was too late. "Actually, I can. It's in the Twenty-Fifth Amendment."

"But why?" Granberry asked again.

"Because all I wanted was to show you I was good enough to be president," I said. "And that's . . . not a good enough reason to be president."

"Wait," Granberry said. "Why would you need to show us you were good enough? And what do you mean by 'good enough'?"

"You think we don't think you're good enough?" Dad said.

I looked him straight in the eye. "I saw you checking your phone at my magic show," I said. "And I heard you on the phone with Mom. I know what you think of me." I looked down. "I know I'm not the kid you wanted."

Dad's mouth dropped open.

"Mike," he said. "Mike. No. You're exactly the kid I wanted. There's no one like you. And that's what makes you special. I'm sorry I checked my phone. And I shouldn't have said those things to your mom. I made a mistake. Do you hear me?"

I nodded. My head felt light, but in a good way, like I'd gotten rid of some of my heavy worries. "What really hurt was you feeling so bad for me," I said. "That's why I wanted to be president."

Dad looked down. "I'm sorry. But why don't you want to be president now?" he asked.

"Because I'm president for the wrong reasons," I said. "I'm only president because I lied. Because I thought it would make people like me. But they don't really like me. They like some fake guy." I looked down. "I had to fake having social skills to win."

"Now hold on a second," said Granberry. "You have your own social skills. Not everybody's are the same. And they don't have to be. All you have to be is true to yourself and kind to others. That's all you need." She took my hand. "Magic is your bridge to other people."

"Here's what I want to know," I said. "Why don't people think magic is cool?"

"I have a theory," Granberry said. "It's because magic requires you to let your guard down. It makes you vulnerable. You have to admit you don't know how everything works, that life can still be surprising and fun. And for some people, that's not cool. And I think that's sad."

She laughed. "Who decides what's cool, anyway? You make the rules. Nobody else."

Dad nodded. "I'll say this: I know how hard it is to feel like you've got to fit in. I did magic when I was your age."

"You did?" I said.

"Of course I did. I was raised by two magicians," he said. "I got teased a lot, though, so I stopped."

"And that was a shame," Granberry said.

"Yes, it was," Dad said. "I guess I just worried you were lonely, Mike. Because I was pretty lonely back then. But you're not me, are you? You're a lot braver than I was."

"No," I said. "I'm not lonely." And I meant it. "When I was being fake, even when I was around other people, that's when I felt lonely."

"I've felt that way, too," Dad said quietly. "You're lucky to have a real passion. That's more than a lot of people ever have." He paused. "I'm sorry if I pushed you too hard to make friends. I wasn't being a very fungal dad."

I smiled. "That's okay," I said. "If you hadn't, I might not be friends with Amelia."

"And I might have pushed you too hard to like chamomile tea," Granberry said.

I laughed.

"I actually like chamomile tea," I said. "But now that we're telling the truth, I don't really like video games."

"Now that we're telling the truth, I bought that console for myself," Dad said. "Can I have it?"

I laughed so hard tears streamed down my face.

"I'm proud of you for being president," Granberry said. She stroked my hair. "For one day. And I'm even prouder that you're quitting."

NOTICE OF EMERGENCY SEVENTH-GRADE CONGRESS!

❖❖❖❖❖❖❖❖❖❖

Monday at lunch in the cafeteria

Called by your new seventh-grade class president,
Mike . . . the Unusual

26

MIKE

A magician is never supposed to reveal their secrets. But lately I hadn't been such a great magician. So today, I, Mike the con artist, was going to break the magician's code in front of the whole seventh-grade class. I'd tell everyone what really happened.

Before I started the meeting, I saluted Peter. He saluted me back.

I'd met him at his locker before school to apologize. He shook my hand. "Let's rebrand this friendship. Team Mike the Unusual is back in business," he'd said.

I cleared my throat.

"Thank you all for attending this emergency meeting of the Seventh-Grade Congress," I said.

"Well, we kind of had to come," Clover said. "It's lunch."

"Make it fast, I'm starving!" said Brayden Monk.

"Respect your president," said Scott.

"I'm starving, Mr. President," said Brayden.

"I want everyone to see who you elected," I said. "Or didn't elect. I only won by default. But this is the real me." I nodded at Peter.

"Presto!" I said, throwing a handful of gold and silver confetti in the air.

The audience oohed. As the confetti fell, Peter helped me put on Granbobby's old coat with tails and his magic hat. Then he handed me my magic wand.

"I'm a magician. Well, I used to be. I turned into a con artist. I misdirected your trust to get votes. That's bad," I said. "So I'm resigning. I don't deserve to be president."

"Huh?" said Alan Firenza. The room buzzed liked a bunch of confused bees.

"I'm sorry," I said. "Most of all, I'm sorry to Clover. I'm the one who vandalized my posters. And I didn't say anything when people accused her."

Clover gasped, leaning back like I'd just called her some mean name. She looked hurt. Betrayed. Maybe that's how I looked when I heard Dad talking on the phone. I hated being the person that hurt somebody else. Clover never did anything wrong. She didn't deserve this.

The audience started booing.

"Wait, all that stuff on your posters was true?" Alan Firenza asked.

I nodded.

It was like I was having a bad show, so bad it confused people and made them mad at the same time. I wanted my headphones. But this wasn't the time for a magic mindset. This was real life. Elections had consequences, and I had to face them.

"What about your girlfriend?" asked Mel Chang, holding up her phone to record my answer.

"Hey, where did you come from?" Brayden Monk asked. "This is seventh-grade lunch. You're in eighth grade."

"I have a press pass. Duh," said Mel.

"No girlfriend," I said. "My only stable relationship is with magic."

Clover gasped.

"So who's president now?" Thalia Jung asked.

"No one!" said Pepper Kowalski. "Anarchy!"

"Eek!" said Seema Singh. She hid under a table.

"I declare myself president!" Big TOE said.

"You can't do that," yelled Mateo Medina.

"I'm swearing myself in now," said Big TOE, holding his left hand up and his right hand over his phone.

I waved my magic wand. "Chatty crowd tonight!" I said in my Mike the Microphone voice, without even thinking about it. I froze, but then a few kids started laughing.

I stood up straighter. "The new president should be the runner-up in the election," I said. "But since Clover dropped out, and there's no vice president, there's no precedent for this. We have to nominate someone else. It's in the Twenty-Fifth Amendment."

I stole a quick look at Amelia out of the corner of my eye. She was smiling, just a little.

"What's the Twenty-Fifth Amendment?" asked Scott.

"It's in the Constitution," I said.

"Yeah, I've heard of that," Scott said.

I uncapped a dry erase marker. "The floor is open for nominations," I said.

"And totally covered with confetti," Rachel said, looking around.

Scott raised his hand. "Anita Tinkle."

Everyone laughed.

Big TOE raised his hand. "Another vote for Anita Tinkle."

"One more!" said Brayden Monk.

"Ugh, you're so immature," said Seema Singh. "What about someone with presidential style. Rafael X?"

"Excellent choice," said Peter. "But is he in the seventh grade?"

We looked around the cafeteria.

"Yeah, I thought he was in eighth," said Mateo Medina.

Mel shrugged. "I've never actually seen him. I've only seen his vids. And he's always in the shadows on camera."

"That's so he doesn't distract from his art," Peter explained.

"My sister said he was doing makeup when she was here," said Pepper Kowalski. "And she's in high school now."

"Wait," said Holly Herman. "Has anyone actually *ever* seen Rafael X?"

The whole cafeteria went silent.

"Hold on," I said. "So our nominees are Anita

Tinkle and Rafael X, who may or may not be a real student."

"I nominate . . . Bobby Odor," said Brayden Monk, snickering.

"You only like Bobby Odor because he's a boy," said Seema Singh.

"People," Clover said. "Anita Tinkle is not real. Bobby Odor is not real. Rafael X . . . maybe? I'm confused about that, because there is definitely a person in those makeup videos."

"He could be a robot," said Holly Herman.

"Anita Tinkle isn't real," Rachel cut in. "But she's a symbol."

"Huh?" Peter said. "Is this one of your bookwriting things?"

Rachel stood up. "Our election was not legitimate," she said. "We never even voted! And nominating Anita Tinkle shows we're mad about that. We'd rather have a fake president with a funny name than a real one who might lie and trick us."

"Hey, I'd like to be a real president," said Eliza Crabtree. "But I can't do stuff after school."

"And I can't run because I got into too much trouble," said Thalia.

"And I can't give speeches," mumbled Demetrius Doran. "I stutter when I get nervous."

Huh. I never knew Demetrius stuttered.

Amelia wiggled in her seat and raised her hand. I nodded.

"Maybe elections, the way people usually do them, don't work anymore," Amelia said. "Maybe it's time for something new."

"Like what?" I asked.

She stood up. "A revolution."

THE POPLAR MIDDLE SCHOOL
SEVENTH-GRADE CONSTITUTION

ℓℓℓℓℓℓ

We the People of the seventh-grade class of Poplar Middle School, in order to form a more perfect union, don't want a class president.

Our election this year was messed up. There was cheating and lying, and people got hurt. The election system, in this seventh-grade class's opinion, is broken.

We want to fix it, so we wrote our own constitution:

- Leaders don't have to be presidents, and anyone can be a leader.
- Every voice is important.
- Power to the people, not the person.

PROPOSAL

Instead of an election, We the People think the seventh-grade student government should be an elective, just like French, drama, or art. An elective will let more kids get involved in making decisions. We the People propose the Anita Tinkle Elective.

ℓℓℓℓℓ

The Anita Tinkle Elective:

✌ Will change the existing class election system, which leaves out almost all students from the political process

💪 Will meet during school hours, so more students can participate, and making it an elective means we can use class time to actually fix problems

✍ Will teach *all* students how to be leaders

ℓℓℓℓℓ

What's New with
Mel Chang

———— ⸨ ————

If It Trends, We're Friends.

POWER PEEPS

LAST NIGHT THE SEVENTH GRADERS ASKED THE SCHOOL BOARD TO ADD THE ANITA TINKLE ELECTIVE TO THE CURRICULUM.

First there was a passionate speech by Amelia Flem. Then Thalia Jung. Then Clover O'Reilly. And Seamus Henry, out of nowhere. Who knew he could stay awake that long? Then Ms. Adamlee, sporting chic American flag earrings, spoke up to support the elective. She even cried. Way to go, teach!

The school board voted, and the final vote was cast by newly elected school board member Mrs. O'Reilly (Clover's mom). The board agreed to add the elective if the students would change the name to the Student Body Elective.

After a dramatic internal meeting, the students agreed to the compromise (mostly because Amelia Flem pointed out that they could still call the elective Anita Tinkle when there were no adults around).

MY BAD

🔊 Let this serve as an offish apology to Holly Herman, who correctly ID'd Mike as the PosterGate vandal. And congrats to Holly for being the newest pres of the Poplar Middle Crimesolvers.

🔊 I'd also like to offer an offish sorry/not-sorry semi-apology to the sixth and eighth graders. I know I've been focusing a lot on seventh graders. I'm not leaving you out on purpose. TBH, you guys need to be more exciting. I'm a reporter. I go where the action is.

INVITATION TO WELCOME ARCH MAKEOVER

by Clover O'Reilly

WHAT: The Welcome Arch Makeover!

WHO'S INVITED: EVERYONE! That's the whole point!

WHERE: The Welcome Arch at Poplar Middle School (it hasn't moved, because it's hard to move an arch)

WHEN: Tomorrow at 7:50 a.m., before the first bell

WHY: The Welcome Arch has always welcomed students to Poplar Middle School. But honestly, the Random Acts of Artness Club was just using it to show off their art skills. Which they should, because we are mega-talented! But still, it wasn't super welcoming.

The new and improved Welcome Arch will be a creative space for everyone in our school. So without further ado, here's a sneak peek of some makeover highlights!

- ✿ The arch will now be a collage, layered with student pictures, notes, sketches, whatever! Shared "heart supplies" will be provided to help everyone express themselves.

- ✿ Check out the giant 3-D cat ear sculpture mail slot, right beside the arch. You can leave direct, anonymous notes to the eighth-grade student council AND school administration.

And get hyped for a fungal celebrity guest to dedicate the new arch to the student body. We're trying for Rafael X, but don't get your hopes up.

27

Clover

It was the day we had to declare our final electives.

"What are you taking, Clover?" Rachel asked as we walked to school. We hadn't shrunk or anything, but the sidewalk seemed less crowded.

"Definitely art," I said. It was tough to decide between art and the new Student Body Elective, but art is my heart. Plus, I realized you can be a changemaker *and* an artist, which is like the perfect combination for me. Plus *plus*, I convinced the studio art teacher to do a unit on Art and Activism.

"What about you, Amelia?" I asked.

"Anita Tinkle," she said. "I mean, the Student Body Elective!"

"You're practically squealing!" I said.

"Well, I'm excited to get back in the game!" she said, wiggling as she walked.

Amelia's "retirement" didn't last very long. I guess being a wonk is *her* heart.

"Thalia's taking it, too," I said. "She wants to design reusable water bottles with our school logo on them. She's also lobbying Dr. Dana to fix the sanitary machines in the girls' bathroom so she doesn't have to punch them."

In a flash, Peter Gronkowski ran across the street. I swear he has hearing like my supersonic smelling. He handed me a business card.

"Those water bottles sound like a great fit for the new and improved school store," he said.

Mike and Scott jogged across the street to catch up with him. "Come on, Peter," Mike said. "They haven't even had their coffee yet." I wasn't even allowed to drink coffee, but he said it in a funny voice, which made me laugh. When someone is funny, it makes them extra cute. Even though I was still kind of mad at Mike for lying, I guess my crush didn't disappear completely.

"Rachel?" Amelia asked.

"I'm sticking with French," she said. She pouted. "I'll miss you, Amelie!"

"You guys know your French names are basically the same as your real names, right?" I said.

They both gave me "find your filter" looks. But then they laughed.

"What are you taking, Scott?" Amelia asked.

He patted a baby doll that was strapped against his chest in a sling. "I'm staying with Family and Consumer Sciences," he said. "I can't abandon my daughter."

"Mike?" I asked.

"Public speaking," he said.

"He's got a magic gig next weekend," Peter said. "As his mentor, I advised him to work on his putter."

"Patter," Mike corrected him. "Yeah, I'm doing a show at Town Hall with Granberry. The first grandson/grandmother performance in Poplar history. I'm her assistant." He smiled proudly.

"Wait," I said. "Your grandma is a magician?! That's the coolest! Can she be our celebrity guest at the Welcome Arch dedication?"

"I'll ask her," he said. He waved as he ran to catch up with Peter and Scott.

Rachel grabbed my arm. "Clover, did you see his wrist?"

I squinted down the block, and my heart almost stopped. Mike was wearing a PROUD BOY LADYBUG bracelet.

"I seriously cannot be expected to concentrate on school today," I said.

Amelia giggled. "How's the design for the book cover coming along?" she asked me. Amelia and I are writing a guide to student government. Rachel is the editor. She's making a press kit and everything to promote it.

"I'm still marinating ideas," I said. "But I'll work on it during office hours today, when I'm not thinking about Mike wearing my bracelet."

My "office hours" aren't really in an office. Dahlia and I are trying a new plan. We each get to have "a room of our own" for one hour each day. Dahlia needs her space, too. It's not so bad. I'm even getting used to the pickle smell.

"What about you? Any ideas for our logo?" I asked Amelia. "I want something bold and different. Something that's never been seen before!"

"I'm the wonk. You're the artist."

I pictured my Dream Room Inspiration Folder and all the new color combinations and textures and patterns I'd imagined to make it special.

I smiled. I was still an artist, even if I didn't have my own room yet.

"A swirl," I said.

MYSTIC MAYHEM MAGIC CAMP
ESSAY

Name: Michael "Mike the Unusual" Strange

Question: How have you achieved the impossible with your magic?

I tried to achieve the impossible and get elected class president. To win, I thought I had to disappear. I lied about who I was to make people think I was cool.

And I won. I guess you could say I achieved the impossible, but it was just a confidence trick. The truth is, I've never done anything impossible with magic. But I know somebody who did.

Her name is Selena Strange. Growing up, she read books about coin magic and linking rings and card tricks. She even learned how to read minds! Still, Selena never saw anyone like her, a black girl, doing magic for an audience. Sometimes she felt like it wasn't even possible.

But she kept working, and she succeeded. People called her an assistant, but she did a lot more than that. She came up with new tricks and made props and designed costumes. She even wrote a book.

Selena Strange is my Granberry. I'm sad that she never got to have a role model growing up. But thanks to her, I do. I'm not sure I'll ever do anything impossible like she did. But she inspires me to try to do what feels impossible to me, even if it's easy for somebody else.

That's why I'm learning close-up magic. I used to think I could only do stage magic. Up close, people can see your mistakes. They might laugh at you and not with you. But that's okay, because I'm a comedy magician. Laughter is part of the gig.

28

MIKE THE UNUSUAL

My eyes were closed. I drowned out all the cafeteria smells and noise and focused on my breath. In, out. In, out.

Someone tapped me on the shoulder. I took off my headphones. It was Peter.

"Are you ready?" he asked.

I nodded, sipping my chamomile tea.

Mom and Dad decided they would pay for Mystic Mayhem Magic Camp if I got in. But I still had to get in. I'd written my essay. Now was the hard part: performing my "achieve the impossible" trick on video.

Today I was trying something new: cafeteria magic. It's my version of close-up magic, where you do magic, but not on a stage. You go up to people and do tricks right in front of them.

Peter was setting up his phone on some kind of stick so he could follow me around the cafeteria.

Poplar Middle School is changing. It seemed to happen pretty soon after the new government elective started. And the changes aren't just regular stuff like more recycling and fund-raisers and pep rallies, even though that's part of it.

The real difference is in the cafeteria. There are still the same number of seats at the tables, but kids are starting to move around more. They don't seem so stuck inside their boxes.

I stretched out my fingers and wiggled them around a little bit. My heart thudded, but I knew I could do it because I was already doing it. I was walking across the cafeteria without my headphones.

They flopped around my neck. I wasn't even trying to look like a cool DJ. They were there just in case I needed them.

I went up to Alan Firenza, who was playing with his magic eight ball.

"Hey, Alan," I said. "Want to see a trick?" I was starting with a warm-up before I moved on to my main event: the Thumb Fan. That was the trick I'd messed up at the Pancake Jamboree. When you make a mistake in magic, the only thing left to do is recover.

Alan nodded.

I held out my hand. "Pick a card, any card."

Acknowledgments

————o————

As always, thanks to all my families (Jones, LeReche, Mincks, and Ross) for their love and support. Thanks to my agent, Steve Malk, for always keeping things in perspective. Thanks to Laura Park, Ken Wright, and the entire Viking team for supporting this second Poplar adventure. Special thanks to my editor, Joanna Cárdenas, for helping me push through political despair to celebrate the joyful spirit of activism embodied by kids all over the world.

Thanks to Michael and Hannah Ammar for sharing their fascinating wisdom and experiences in the magic world; my father-in-law Rick Ross for talking through trick logistics (and for Meredith's patience!); my brother-in-law Nick LeReche for his middle-school savvy and commitment to creative, progressive education; my mother-in-law Terri Ross and Van Galyon for their generosity in caring for Mattie; Chelsea Beam for her valuable feedback; and Scott, Mattie, and Reesie for the group hugs.